GREETINGS FROM FEARSBURG

Fearsburg, of all places! My crooks couldn't have chosen a nice city-state like Lost Cause City, Scavengerburg, or No Hope Juncture, where they at least give you a square meal before they shoot you.

The only lights come from the dim streetlamps and neon signs. One showed a giant ear. The caption read: LOOSE TALK KILLS. Another pictured a huge eye: WATCH YOUR NEIGHBOR. A third simply said OBEY. It flashed on and off in the empty street as if daring someone to disagree. There were no takers. Everyone was hiding out indoors. Except us, of course.

If nothing else, I'd learned one small thing: why they call this Fearsburg. I'd been here only a few minutes and already I was afraid...

Other Books by
Isidore Haiblum
Coming Soon from Avon Books

CRYSTALWORLD

SPECTERWORLD

Isidore Haiblum

AVON BOOKS NEW YORK

SPECTERWORLD is an original publication of Avon Books. This work has never before appeared in book form. This work is a novel. Any similarity to actual persons or events is purely coincidental.

AVON BOOKS
A division of
The Hearst Corporation
1350 Avenue of the Americas
New York, New York 10019

Copyright © 1991 by Isidore Haiblum
Cover art by Gary Ruddell
Published by arrangement with the author
Library of Congress Catalog Card Number: 91-91787
ISBN: 0-380-75858-X

First Avon Books Printing: August 1991

AVON TRADEMARK REG. U.S. PAT. OFF. AND IN OTHER COUNTRIES, MARCA REGISTRADA, HECHO EN U.S.A.

Printed in the U.S.A.

RA 10 9 8 7 6 5 4 3 2 1

CHAPTER 1

We rolled into Cashville eight-thirty at night.

Good old Cashville, I'd lost enough dough on their stock markets to retire twice over. Finally, something *nice* was going to happen here. Maybe.

I gave the streets an appraising glance.

Everyone in Cashville kept banker's hours. The place, at this hour, was as bare as a wallet on Poverty Row, only a helluva lot cleaner. Right away I regretted the rotten comparison. The mere thought of Poverty Row instantly depressed me—I never could stand the sight of starving people.

Here, fortunately, was something else: narrow cobble-stoned streets, old-fashioned lampposts, and giant glass-and-aluminum buildings reaching skyward, as if trying to poke their way into better, friendlier climes. Who could blame them? Everything was spick-and-span. A real tribute to the automat cleaning system, if nothing else.

Cashville, where big money changed hands.

My job: to see that the hands were the right ones. Nothing to it. Especially if you were a hotshot and had the right help. I'd made sure about the latter part at least.

I pulled up on a side street. "Okay, gang," I said to the talkie button in my lapel, "this is it."

"Aye aye, skipper," a mech voice replied.

Behind me the convoy of trucks and vans came to a sudden halt.

I climbed out of my heap, Seymore Salent right at my heels. The little guy was as tough to shake as the common cold. And about as much fun to have around.

"Just keep out of everyone's way, Salent," I said, "and maybe you won't get hurt."

"Hurt? Bite your tongue, Dunjer. How can I make your name a household word if I land in the emergency ward?"

"Forget the household word," I told him. "I'll settle for vague recognition."

This Salent was a small man in a brown double-breasted suit, green polka-dot bow tie, and white shirt. Brown eyes peered out from behind thick round glasses. Curly brown hair of a darker shade hung over his collar and brow. He had a large nose, no doubt helpful in sniffing out news, or what passed for news on the pages of the *Daily Tattler*. Salent was the rag's chief snoop, the guy who was going to put my outfit, Security Plus, on the map. My mental condition must've been verging on dementia when I let him talk me into bringing him along. But if I gave him his walking papers now, all the publicity I'd be getting would be negative, and I already had plenty of that.

Meanwhile, the trucks and vans were disgorging hordes of mechs, my agency's prime operatives. The thing about mechs is that they can't be bribed, a real plus in Happy City, and most of the other city-states, as well. Mechs don't need wages, either, don't require sick leave, and almost never quit in a huff. Aside from an occasional oiling and the danger of internal rot, the only thing wrong with mechs is that they're mechs. Wrong enough in my book, but who'd be dumb enough to bite the hand that feeds him—especially if it's made of metal?

XX21 came over, gave me a brisk salute. "We take our positions now, boss?"

"Yeah. We're a couple hours early, but our guests may arrive ahead of schedule."

"Got it, chief."

"And keep awake," Salent said, a broad grin on his face.

We both ignored him. The mechs silently faded off into the night. There were shooter mechs and spotter mechs and chaser mechs. And a half dozen double Xs like XX21 to keep them on their toes. Even if they didn't have any toes.

"Where they going?" Salent asked, pen and notebook out.

"To blanket the area. Some'll be in the surrounding buildings, others right here in offices of the Exchange itself. And a few are lookouts up on the roofs. Everything's sewn up tight."

"By the mechs?"

I nodded.

"So how come you're even here?"

"To take the credit, what else?" I said. "*Someone's* got to."

I sat back in a swivel chair, my feet up on an empty desk. Salent had parked himself on the sofa. We both watched the monitor the installation mech had thoughtfully installed. At the moment it showed nothing more interesting than the unlit office five doors down the hall. But I had hopes.

"That's where they keep the negotiable bonds," I told Salent. "Nothing like a negotiable bond to brighten one's life, eh? We've got spotter eyes on all the doors, lifts, and out in the hallway. We've planted catcher ears, too. Naturally, it's all videotaped and recorded, so when it goes to trial the case'll be airtight."

"Crime *really* doesn't pay," Salent said.

"Yeah, but don't let the word get around. It might be bad for business."

* * *

Our visitors showed up some two hours later, right on schedule. They made enough racket jimmying the back door to deafen the catcher ear. Luckily, they'd been smart enough to find and cut the alarm wires or the city constables might've nabbed 'em before they even got to my floor, a hateful thought if ever there was one.

Four men in ski masks appeared in the two-inch monitor display square. The rest of the tube still showed the darkened office. Spotter eyes followed the foursome's progress as they cautiously made their way through the basement and into the speed lift. Two of the party wore jackets and peaked caps. The other pair had on long coats and hats pulled low over their foreheads. All four wore gloves.

"Typical criminal attire," I told Salent. "Gotta dress like that or they take your union card away. Only thing missing is the guns. Probably got those stashed in their pockets. That's why it's important to have mechs around. Shoot one of them, they hardly notice."

The speed lift had stopped on our floor. Spotter eyes tracked our desperadoes as they moved toward us down the hall.

"Why don't you grab them now?" Salent whispered.

"Because breaking and entering is a minor offense," I whispered back. "Nailing two-bit thieves is hardly big-league gumshoeing, is it? Wouldn't rate five lines in your sheet."

"Three maybe."

"Safecracking," I said with some satisfaction, "is something else."

The four guys didn't waste any time once they hit their destination. We got an eyeful of their efforts via the large screen. It included locating the safe behind its partition—a real necessity if you're going to swipe what's inside—and using an old-fashioned electric decoder on the combination locks. I sighed. My big-time crooks were acting like amateurs.

"Watch closely," I told Salent. "In case you ever change professions."

"And become a safecracker?"

"Yeah. This'll teach you what *not* to do."

"You're a real sport, Dunjer."

I waved away the compliment. "All in a day's work, Seymore."

"So what shouldn't I do?"

"Use antiquated decoders for one thing. That gizmo's been passé for years. Wasn't too hot in its heyday either. Second, don't take more than a few minutes getting in and out, you're liable to get caught. As I'll demonstrate in a moment. Or, rather, the mechs will. Credit where credit is due, eh? That's not for publication, Salent."

One of the guys must have noticed that the decoder wasn't doing the trick because he reached into his coat pocket and pulled out two sticks of dynamite. He waved them around as if daring the damn things to go off, right there in his paw.

"Make that half a moment. Move!" I hissed at my lapel button.

One thing about mechs, you don't have to tell 'em twice.

Almost instantly the door banged open and the room on the screen was filled with mechs. Most thieves call it quits when confronted by a squad of intrepid metal men, and these birds were no exception. They raised their hands high and stood perfectly still. A lot smarter than trying to blow us all up. I was glad to see *some* smarts. These lads were beginning to worry me.

"Come on, Salent," I said, getting to my feet. "Let's see what we've got."

The pint-sized reporter followed me five doors down the hall to where the action was—if that was the right term for a lot of immobile mechs and people with their hands in the air.

"Hi, gang," I said.

XX21 gave me a snappy salute. "All's shipshape, skipper. They offered no resistance."

"Shows they're not crazy," I said. "So at least they won't be able to plead insanity. Okay, fellas," I said, turning to our suspects, "put your hands down and pull off those face masks."

"By cracky," one of them said, "it's a live one."

"Knew we'd hit pay dirt this time," his pal said.

Four masks were peeled away. I did a double take. I was looking at four oldsters who couldn't've been a day under eighty-five. Seamy faces. Toothless gums. Bald pates. Here was a walking ad for an old-age home.

"These your desperadoes?" Salent asked.

"Yippee," one of the miscreants called out. "The Old-Timers' Gang rides again!"

"That's what you call yourselves," I said in some wonder, "the Old-Timers' Gang?"

"Sure, by jiminy. Why beat about the bush? We're *old*, sonny, ain't no two ways about it."

"And you crack safes?" I asked.

"We try, Junior."

"Ain't rightly cracked one in a coon's age," one of his buddies said.

"But we keeps at it. Yes-sirree."

"Hope to strike it rich, huh?" Salent said accusingly, as if the mere thought were crime enough.

"Tarnation, we ain't *that* dumb, sonny."

"Crime don't pay," another oldster cackled. "My mummy told me that."

"So how come you do it?" Salent demanded.

"Best way to land in the pokey, that's why."

"Once you get pinched," the fourth duffer said, "you're hoosegow-bound; whoopee!"

"You *want* to get caught?" Salent said.

"Ain't no place like the calaboose."

His chum licked his lips. "They still got them tasty hominy grits in the jug?"

"Can't beat the chow, boy. They serve three square *every* day."

"An' you gets your shut-eye on a *real* mattress."

"Ain't no place like the cooler for downright comfort."

Salent turned a withering eye my way. "Some master-minds of crime."

"They came highly recommended," I said.

"By *whom*, Dunjer, the local geriatric clinic?"

"The stoolie who sent me on this wild goose chase."

"He brain-damaged, or what?"

"What stoolie isn't? But up until now he never gave me a bum steer."

"So what happened?"

"There's always a first time," I said.

CHAPTER 2

"Mr. Dunjer."

"Eh?" I said.

I was alone in the car. Salent had taken off for his office to file his copy. The four felons were tucked away in the Security Plus paddy wagon, which was hauling 'em off to their beloved clink. It was bad enough that most crooks their age had been dead for years. I just hoped they kept their mouths shut about their preference for being safely behind bars; I had enough troubles without becoming the laughingstock of the Happy City precinct house.

I looked at the dashboard communo. "Is that you?" I asked.

"Certainly," the dashboard said. "Who else could it be?"

"You" was the alarm board back at the office. It almost never called me directly when I was in the field. "Something's happened?"

"The noble mechanical is not in the habit of making idle chitchat. *Of course* something has happened."

I turned up a ramp, began going from ground level to high-drive. The spiffy glass towers behind me seemed to twinkle bye-bye, as if even a district devoted solely to finance could have a light side. I wasn't fooled one bit.

Ahead of me was darkness, in more ways than one. No doubt about it, the damn alarm board had done it again, unnerved me. It didn't take much these days.

"So," I asked, "you're not going to tell me?"

"It hardly matters now," it said. "The constables have taken over."

"The constables?"

"Well, you were nowhere to be reached. None of the double Xs was in contact range."

"They were with me."

"There you are." The stupid alarm board actually sounded aggravated. "What was I to do?" it asked.

"You actually called the constables?" I said with some amazement.

"The noble mechanical," the alarm board said, "despite his immobile demeanor, prides himself on a modicum of insight and wisdom, not to mention street smarts. I would hardly summon our arch-rivals to a site guarded by our agency. Truff's foreman called them."

"There's been trouble at Truff's?"

"Certainly there's been trouble at Truff's. What do you think this conversation is about?"

"I was starting to wonder."

"Unauthorized parties invaded the premises less than an hour ago. They absconded with various items of an unknown nature. It is, however, safe to surmise that these items were either money or tools, since that is all there is on the premises."

"What about our spotter eyes?"

"Blinded."

"Catcher ears?"

"Stuffed."

"Just like that?"

"Must I draw the obvious conclusion for you?"

"Spare me. And X30 and X31?"

"They have ceased to function."

I sighed. "Well, it's lucky for us we're out in full force. I'll just signal the old crew and we can scoot on over and see what's what, who's who, and which's which—not to mention just how badly the damn joint's been nicked. No telling how a full mech contingent can come in handy."

"I would not bother," the alarm board said. "It is redundant."

"The constables keep you informed of their moves, do they?" I said coldly.

"The tele-visa does. The networks are out with camera crews. All of Happy City can watch."

"All?"

"As well as the adjoining city-states, the ones that are not jamming us, of course."

"Great. We get any play?"

"Not at first. But Constable Krimshaw did happen to say that the Tool Works was our responsibility."

"He did?" That wasn't so hot.

"Eighteen times."

"That many?"

"Perhaps more. I have stopped counting since our talk began."

"Uh huh. Maybe I'd just better mosey over there myself."

"It would certainly seem to be the recommended course," the alarm board said. "Remember to smile if you get on camera."

Truff's Tool Works covered a five-block radius. The whole area was roped off, the streets barricaded against the crush of spectators who'd come to take in the sights—and some sights they were! The Happy City Carnival was never as festive. The only thing missing were the guys selling tickets and the hot-dog vendors; they couldn't be far behind.

Cops were all over the joint as though the Policemen's Ball were being held in the Tool Works this year. Searchlights sent long columns of light into the darkness, illuminating factory buildings and the sky above. Copters buzzed overhead. The Happy City Zeppelin was on the scene, the usual commercials lighting up its sides: EAT STEROID-SNAPS—GROW PLENTY BIG! BE CLASSY, WEAR ZOOT-SUIT DUDS! TURN ON WITH SPUNKY COLA! BLISS OUT ON NARCO SMOKES! REELECT KRIMSHAW CHIEF CONSTABLE, FEEL SAFE! Good old Krimshaw, he didn't miss a trick, at least when it came to plugging himself. The only way to feel safe with that guy was to lock him up somewhere. But with three P.R. outfits working overtime for the constable, who would believe it? The Tri-D networks did their part. They were in full display just now—camera crews getting the red carpet treatment—on both sides of the barricades. Some of the copters were network, too. For Krimshaw to've pulled all the stops like this, the bad guys must've been sitting ducks.

I double-parked, put my talkie in synch with the car's communo so I could get messages directly from the field, as long as I stayed in range, hung an M.D. sign on my windshield, a NO RADIO, NO TELE-VISA, NO LIQUOR CABINET sign on the side window, magno-locked and electrified the door handles, and began squeezing my way through the crush. Backs, elbows, shoulders, knees, and stomachs got in my way, tried to check my progress, keep me from an undeserving close-up view. Twice, I had to pry a hand off the wallet in my back pocket; I like to leave charity to the proper institutions. By the time I hit the barricade, I was ready to call it quits and skedaddle for home. The only thing stopping me was the thought of working my way through the damn crush again.

"Hold it, bud." A large cop stood between me and the Tool Works gate. "You with the press?"

I gave him a no.

"Only the press gets in," he said.

I told him who I was.

The cop sighed, spoke into his talkie button. We waited while I got dirty looks from the crowd around us. After a while the button spoke back. The cop nodded and waved me through. Someone booed.

Two guys were waiting for me on the other side of the gate to escort me up the block. "Constables?" I asked.

"P.R.," one guy said. It figured.

We went by a couple of darkened factories, turned a corner, and there was the command post.

Giant klieg lights, Tri-D cameras, and scurrying techs bore down on a dozen persons. I recognized the constabulary top brass, Miss Happy City of last year who'd become a Tri-D interviewer, and a trio of her male rivals from the other networks. I was sorry I hadn't brought my makeup kit like everyone else.

It took a while for Krimshaw to free himself of his official duties, which at the moment consisted of posing for the cameras, and join me.

The constable waddled over and pumped my hand. He was dressed in a blue and gold tunic. Gold sandals adorned his feet. A large gold star with three ribbons hung on his left breast. A black cartridge belt and holster was tied around his ample midriff. He was six-three and weighed in at over the three hundred mark. His face was oval, black hair sparse, nose and lips large. A double chin bounced up and down at the slightest excuse. His eyes were steel-gray, but at the moment well-hidden behind dark glasses.

"Never a dull moment, huh, Dunjer?" he boomed at me.

I had to admit it. "Crime knows no holiday, Krimshaw," I said grimly.

"Crime? Who said anything about crime? I'm talking about those blasted interviewers. It's no breeze under those klieg lights, Dunjer. Next thing you know, they'll be asking me about my toilet habits."

"Not getting personal, are they?"

"Quit kidding, Dunjer. Why, one of them actually wanted to know why I'd taken a vacation last month. As though I didn't have one coming." There was a noticeable whine in the constable's voice.

"Sixth one this year, isn't it?" I said.

"Seventh. And not a damn moment too soon. Job takes a lot out of a man, Dunjer. This constant wrangling with criminals can wear you down just like that." He snapped his fingers.

"Not me, Krimshaw; I let mechs do my wrangling for me."

He gave me a half-grin. "Well, actually, my staff does most of the wrangling. But they report back to me; I'm not spared one grueling detail. It takes its toll, Dunjer."

"Yeah, you look emaciated with worry, pal."

"Let's not get vulgar. Truff's Tool Works was your baby. You got the contract to keep it safe from crime. And look what's happened."

"Exactly what *has* happened?" I asked with some interest.

"Crime, Dunjer. Dastardly, disorderly crime. Somewhere in those tool works, in the labyrinthine factories, underground storage areas, sprawling executive offices," Krimshaw gestured toward the darkened buildings, "we have trapped a band of outlaws who will stop at nothing to get their way."

"And what's that, Krimshaw?"

He shrugged a massive shoulder. "Who knows? We'll find that out when we nail 'em."

"What happened to my mechs?"

The chief constable gave me a broad grin. "Maybe they were on their coffee break."

"Yeah, coffee break. Tell me one thing, Krimshaw."

"Sure, Dunjer."

"How come you gad about in that dumb outfit?"

"Dumb? Outfit? This? Why, it's the very latest style."

"Maybe. But not exactly practical for nabbing bad guys, is it?"

The chief constable shrugged. "For nabbing bad guys, Dunjer, for chasing, shooting, or clubbing, for giving the third degree, I employ a large staff of paid professionals, the best that taxpayers' money can buy. This outfit is for being interviewed on Tri-D. Don't you know anything?''

''I'm learning.''

''It's never too late, Dunjer. These days, the taxpayers expect their public servants to be celebrities. When a thing like this happens, a bona fide big knock-over, the public wants to see its chief constable on the scene, in charge, and looking good. That's why I've held off with the pinch.''

''Held off?''

''Sure. We've had them bottled up for an hour now. Have to give the tele-visa audience out there a chance to grow, to reach its peak.''

''You're in a tough racket, Krimshaw.''

''Darn tootin'. Now's about the right time, wouldn't you say?''

''Wait any longer your boys'll want time and a half.''

Krimshaw looked grave. ''You've got a point there, Dunjer.'' He spoke into the talkie stuck behind his gold star. ''Flush 'em out, boys.''

Almost at once I heard firing, handguns, automatic weapons. Something that sounded like dynamite went off. Flares lit up the night sky, for an instant turned it into bright day.

Krimshaw grinned. ''Media likes a good show.''

''Shouldn't you be in front of the cameras, pal?''

''An important technical question, Dunjer, one that goes to the very heart of being chief constable. Answer's no. Not till they land the rascals. It's best the tele-visa viewers think I'm leading the charge.''

''Best for whom?''

''Me, of course. I can do without the sarcasm, Dunjer.''

It didn't take long for Krimshaw's talkie to beep. ''Got them, Chief.''

''Where in tarnation are you, boys?''

''Front of the main warehouse.''

''Sit tight till I join you.'' To me he said, ''Gotta go, Dunjer.''

Krimshaw, good as his word, waddled off. I stared after

him as he vanished into the shadows. This definitely wasn't going to be one of my better days. Not only was I going to make the *Tattler*'s front page with my bunch of over-the-hill toughs, a surefire laugh riot for most of Happy City, but I was going to get another black eye over this Tool Works break-in. And old crooked Krimshaw would garner all the credit for the dumb bust. I was far too grown-up to feel bitter about a little thing like that. So how come I felt bitter?

I made my way over to the media circle. Inspector McGregor was basking under the bright lights, reeling off a list of public enemies the department had collared. My depression was growing by leaps and bounds. Maybe there really *was* no justice? A helluva note for a crime-fighter, although, actually, I was more in the security line myself.

I made sure to station myself behind a tall guy so I couldn't be seen by the reporters. I make it a habit never to eat crow after eight-thirty. Especially in public.

The interviewer broke off in mid-sentence, leaving the inspector with his mouth half-open, a familiar enough sight.

"Folks," Rudolph Swinch, the late-night anchor, called out excitedly to his many Tri-D faithful, "the Channel Y News Copter has just sent me a flash. Chief Constable Krimshaw, a group of deputies, and three unidentified men are, at this very moment, making their way to a side exit here at the Truff Tool Works. Wait, here's the Tri-D image now."

I couldn't see the monitor, but suddenly I was feeling better, almost chipper. For Krimshaw to be sneaking out, something bad must've happened. Bad for *him*.

Swinch hollered, "Folks, I don't have to tell you, the constable's well-known for his shyness, modesty, and humility—for his penchant for ducking the limelight. He's just made another brilliant arrest, but is he going to show up here in the Tri-D circle and take his bow? Is he going to get the applause he so richly deserves? You bet he is. Even if he doesn't want it! Come on, folks!"

The media crews, mobile lights, and cameras took off with the crowd at their heels. Overhead, the news copters swooped down as though they were going to bomb the place—not a bad idea. I moved with the crowd.

The constable must've heard us coming because he tried to make a run for it. The poor sap didn't have a prayer, not with half the Happy City news hounds after him.

They caught him and his party at the southwest gate.

The three prisoners Krimshaw was trying to sneak out weren't old codgers like the ones I'd landed. They were in their thirties, if not exactly their prime.

What Krimshaw had nabbed looked like three of Happy City's not so happy hobos.

Probably because that's exactly what they were.

CHAPTER 3

A wall of bodies blocked Krimshaw's little group.

"Stand back, boys," the constable said reasonably. "Let 'em through."

A chorus of unreasonable voices answered him.

"Give us a statement, Sam."

"Don't be a meanie, Chief."

"You're on camera, Sam."

"Whole town's watching, Constable."

These birds sounded more like stooges than reporters; they were being too damn nice. Still, Krimshaw didn't look pleased. That gave me an idea. Why should I be the only goat in town? Making a megaphone of my hands, I bawled, "Let 'em speak, Sam! Whadya afraid of?"

The crowd liked the sound of that. A few voices echoed mine. Others joined them, took up the chant as though there was real wisdom in it. The lot of us made a fine racket, as if we were out at the ballpark razzing the umpire.

Krimshaw's mouth fell open like a busted drawbridge. I almost felt sorry for the big bum. But how sorry can you feel for a guy who drags your outfit through the mud eighteen times?

The nice fuss was dying down. In the sudden silence, I yelled again. "Think of your image, Sam!"

Krimshaw turned beet-red, swiveled his head around frantically to see where the annoying voice was coming from. I ducked behind a fat party.

The fact that the constable wasn't looking his cheerful best didn't escape the crowd. Instantly, they took up the chant: "Image! Image! Image!" Some crowd. They were some fifty deep. But even so, Krimshaw could've handled them—called in riot control, used tear gas, water hoses, the good old billy club, taught the citizens a classic lesson in law and order. Only not with the cameras looking on. That was the catch, all right. So much for the classics.

Krimshaw shrugged, held up a meaty hand, and tried on a smile. "If that's what you want," he said gamely.

The news hawks didn't have to be asked twice, they zeroed in on one of the hobos, a tall scraggly fellow with a three-days' growth of beard. He blinked into the lights, licked his lips, and became an instant celebrity.

"We was just mindin' our own business," he said. "Honest."

"Yes, sir," his pal, a medium-sized guy, put in. "Just tryin' to grab a little shut-eye. Ain't no crime in that."

"No crime," the scraggly one agreed.

The shortest of the three piped up. "Then we heard this racket."

"What kind of racket?" a reporter yelled.

"Sounded like a door bein' broken open. So we hid. Pretty soon these masked guys shows up. They started tossin' tools into this cart, real quick."

"We didn't let outta peep," the tall hobo said. "Got enough trouble."

"Right," the short one said. "They took off lickety-split."

The medium-sized guy said, "Next thing, we heard all this yellin' outside."

"I looked outta window," the tall one said, "and saw there was constables all over the place."

The medium-sized one said, "Didn't do nothin' for an hour, either—"

"That'll do," Krimshaw said.

"Then they all rushed in and grabbed us," the short one said. "As though we was the crooks."

"What do you expect 'em to do?" Krimshaw asked the cameras, smiling weakly. "Confess?"

"*Confess?*" the medium one said.

"So where'd we stash the loot?" the short one demanded.

"Yeah," the tall hobo said. "Ain't nothin' in our pockets but air."

Krimshaw said, "Isn't fair to have these boys shootin' off their yaps like this. Could say something that might incriminate 'em. That's not the Happy City way, is it, my friends? In Happy City everyone has rights, even low-down scum like these shameless rats. So how about letting us pass?"

The crowd didn't stir. But I'd had enough. Today Krimshaw, tomorrow me. What was there to cheer about? I began to pry my way through the crush; a crowbar would've come in handy. My talkie beeped.

"Yeah?" I said.

"Trouble, boss."

"Trouble's my business," I said with simple dignity. On good days I even believed it. This wasn't one of them.

"The Miklib Plant's being knocked over."

"Not *that* much trouble. Who is this?"

"X41, skipper."

"So why don't you stop them?"

"Because they've got missile projectiles, that's why. They could blow me away, chief. I know how much that would set back the company. You won't see *me* jeopardizing a valuable property, like some folks. No sir, boss, when it comes to safeguarding company property, I take a backseat to no one."

"What exactly are you doing?"

"Hiding. Call out the troops, skipper, sound the alarm, this is war!"

"Stay calm, X41, I'll be there in a jiffy."

"The troops, boss, the troops. Not *you*. You they can blow away too."

"Just lay low, X41, we'll *all* be there soon."

"Thank goodness."

I beeped the alarm board. "You heard?"

"Of course I heard. I *am* transmitting it, you know. You have orders?"

"Red alert," I told it. "The Miklib Plant. They've got missile projectiles, so take all due precautions: full shields and battle gear. Advance guard in our copter, the rest on wheels. On the double."

"And *your* mode of transportation?"

"Don't worry about me," I said.

"Well, if you say so. That's certainly a load off my circuits."

"By the way," I said, "just where *is* the Miklib Plant?"

"You don't know? Beyond the city's limits."

"Beyond?"

"Between here and Fearsburg."

"That far? What the hell are we doing over there?"

"Earning a very large fee."

"I knew there was a reason."

"You certainly are having an exciting day."

"I sure am. Over and out."

I looked around. The press conference behind me was still going great guns. The crowd hadn't budged. I began working my way back toward the action. If my first foray through this bunch had engendered outright hostility, my second trip produced sheer murderous rage. I'd expected to get into a brawl, but at the Miklib Plant, not here.

Krimshaw was busy giving a speech when I reached him. The three hobos looked glum. So did the cops and reporters.

I glanced around, hunting for a likely candidate, and

finally settled on Ned Restly, the Channel V crime specialist. He was a big, burly ex–football player with a squarish face under a mop of brown curly hair. He could take care of himself. The only question was whether he'd be dumb enough to risk his life for a scoop.

I edged on over.

"Ned," I said after our handshake, keeping my voice low, "I've got something for you that beats this by miles."

Restly looked from me to the constable. "That's not very hard," he said, "is it?"

"I suppose not. But this would beat the ordinary twelve-car smash up on old 68. Or the usual gang slaughter in Slumlord Haven. It might even outshine wholesale embezzlement on Investment Row."

"It's *that* big?"

"Even bigger, maybe. What would you say," I asked, "if I told you there were some *real* bad guys cleaning out a plant, right now?"

"Is that as in scour with Swifty Cleanser, or as in burglary?" And the big lug grinned at me.

"Krimshaw's spiel has rotted your brains, Ned. This is no joke."

"No joke? Then I'd say call the cops. Easy enough if you can shut this baboon up long enough so he'll listen to you."

"Uh uh. This is one of Security Plus's babies. I just got beeped."

"So what happens?"

"We bag the baddies."

"You inviting me along?"

"I'm inviting you to chauffeur me. That's how you get your scoop."

"Finance unit repossess your car?"

"Car won't do. Only a copter can whisk me to the scene in time."

He looked at me. "*Our* copter's up above."

"Bring it down."

"*Here?*"

"Where else?"

He waved a hand. "The people."

"The sacrifice of the few for the many is an honored tradition."

"Sacrifice? To stop some break-in?"

"It's everyone's duty to stop crime. Besides, I imagine this crowd'll get out of the way, don't you?"

"And the constable?"

"Should shut him up."

"I suppose it should."

"Can't beat that, Ned."

"Guess not," he said.

"So, you game?"

"I can't really turn down a scoop," he said.

"That's what I figured."

"No matter how much I'd like to."

"What I admire most about the press," I said, "is their fighting spirit."

"Let's get this over with, shall we?"

"After you, chum."

CHAPTER 4

"You didn't tell me it was all the way out in the sticks," Restly complained.

"It makes a difference?"

He nodded. "I don't even know if they receive Channel V out here." The guy looked uneasy.

"So what? A scoop's a scoop."

"Not if it's this close to Fearsburg."

"Fearsburg doesn't figure in this," I told him. "Relax, Restly, and enjoy the ride."

He eyed me suspiciously, but settled back in his seat.

We were high up in the Channel V News Copter. Below us stretched Happy City. All we could see was a bunch of multicolored lights, the rest was darkness. From up here, even in daylight, it was tough to tell how happy everyone down there was. It wasn't so easy from down there either.

"Eight minutes to the Miklib Plant," the pilot said.

This pilot was a middle-aged gent with a whiny voice, receding hairline, a wrinkled, worried brow, and bags under his eyes. He sat hunched over his controls as though afraid they might try to give him the slip and escape out of the copter.

I was starting to feel queasy.

"What's the plan, Dunjer?" Restly asked, grinning.

"Plan?"

"You going to zap them? Drill them? Puncture their hides with deadly laser blasts? You going to chop them into little pieces?"

I looked at the guy. "Where'd you get a disgusting idea like that?"

He shrugged. "That's show biz, kid."

"I thought you ran a news program."

"Grow up, Dunjer. These days you have to put on a show for the folks."

"You're confusing me with the circus, Restly. Crime-fighting is serious business."

"Who said it wasn't? How about you jump out of the copter and personally take on the bad guys? A real shoot-out. Our viewers eat that up."

"You can get killed in a shoot-out."

"Try not to, Dunjer. It depresses the viewers when the good guys buy the farm."

"It wouldn't give me much of a lift either. Forget that crap, Restly. One of the advantages of heading up a mech outfit is that your personnel risk life and limb for the old cause, not you."

"You don't say?" Restly said. "They make *me* risk life and limb on this job. There isn't even a mech on the whole channel to send in my place."

"Stiff upper lip, pal," I said. "This is hardly the time for trivial gripes. You're about to see the peerless mech in action, Restly. That's award-winning stuff!"

"Mechs, huh? I don't know, Dunjer—"

"Crank up your camera, Ned. Get the audio mikes tuned in. Switch on that old ultra violet so you can get the full, blissful picture."

"Maybe if there's a lot of violence," he said.

"Hell," I said, "those mechs glory in carnage. Bloodshed's their middle name. Takes a whole crew of char ladies to clean up after 'em."

"If you say so, Dunjer."

"Sure I do, and I'm the expert. And remember, Ned, tell your viewers that Tom Dunjer's out there leading the charge. Citizens like to know there's a human hand on the throttle. That someone with savvy and know-how is calling the shots. That, in short, the situation is under control."

"And that's what you do?"

"No, that's what *they* do. But what the rubes don't know won't hurt them, eh?"

"Five minutes to destination, buddy," the pilot called.

Below us was darkness punctuated by only a few lights now. The city proper was way behind. Here, I knew, were mostly scattered houses, trees, grass, and shrubs. And an occasional factory. The laws against pollution, eighteen-hour workdays, and child labor weren't very tough in Happy City. But out here there were almost no laws at all.

"The plan's a snap," I said. "At this very moment, guys, the Security Plus copter is probably landing at Miklib's, ready to take on the hoods. We've got a couple of mechs in the plant itself to show 'em the way. That's just the advance guard. We've got a fleet of mechs zooming down three different drives. Should get to the plant in jig time. And make mincemeat of the opposition. Any questions?"

"Yeah," the pilot said. "How come I can't spot your guys on the radar?"

"What?" I said.

"They're not there, buddy. See for yourself."

I saw. The screen was as blank as the mind of a dimwit.

"Copter's probably landed already," I explained.

"Let's see," the pilot said.

He flicked a button. Another screen lit up. I could see the terrain below clear as day. "Ultraviolet?" I asked.

"Right, buddy. Now we flick on the long-range magnifier, adjust it to the Miklib co-ords, and what do we see?"

"Nothing yet," I said. "You sure your gadgets are functioning? We don't want to deprive your viewers."

"Give it a chance, buddy."

The screen began to clear. What I saw was a factory.

"Any copters hanging around?" the pilot asked.

"Uh uh."

"It's not that I want to tell you your business, buddy, but I couldn't help overhearing all this loose talk about crooks, burglars, and break-ins. If you got an army of mechs down there, that's one thing. But if it's just you, me, and him against *them*, count me out. All I'm supposed to do is fly this crate. Regulations say I get time and a half for hazardous duty; that means easy stuff like flying through tornadoes and hurricanes. Armed combat is something else. I like to leave that to the regular army. They got the training, buddy, not to mention the extra insurance coverage."

"You said it was going to be a snap, Dunjer," Restly said accusingly. "Wading in *all* alone is for the birds. You can't expect *me* to be part of that."

"Come on, guys," I said. "Let's not panic. We still got a whole minute before we land this thing."

"Let's call the constables," Restly said.

"You mean Krimshaw?" I asked.

"Forget I said that," Restly said.

"Look," the pilot said, "it's okay by me if you both wanna be heroes. I'll be glad to drop you off anywhere outside the range of fire. Only you gotta tell me where."

"Hero?" I said. "Thought's never even crossed my mind."

"When I was being a hero," Restly said, "it was on the football field, and I was being paid big bucks."

I said, "Only there's one small thing I think we ought to note in passing."

"I hope it's something encouraging," Restly said. He sounded gloomy, as though I'd asked him to take on the bad guys while I sacked out in the copter.

"Encouraging enough, pal, at least from a certain angle. Look, no one's firing at us."

"Not yet," the pilot said.

"There's no sign of any weapons there capable of bringing a copter down," I pointed out.

"None on the screen," Restly admitted.

"In fact, there's no sign of *anyone* down there."

"You think they've gone?" Restly asked.

"One way to find out," I said.

By now we were almost directly over the Miklib Plant. The screen showed no vehicles of any kind. No lights shone through the plant windows. There was no movement on the grounds.

I was in range; I beeped the talkie.

"Skipper?" X41 replied.

"They still around?" I asked.

"If you mean the burglars, certainly."

"What're they up to?"

"They appear to be removing a good many items."

"Money? Bonds? Securities? Company records?"

"None of those, chief."

"None?"

"Nary a one."

"So what're they taking?"

"The plant."

"Eh?"

"They appear to be dismantling the plant. Naturally, I can't be sure of their progress. I'm in the basement in a closet. Who would think that in this day and age there are still closets full of old brooms, mops, and dusters?"

"You're in the broom closet?"

"As soon as they leave, skipper, I'll resume my post."

"When they leave it'll be too late," I said. "What happened to X42, he in the coal bin?"

"There is no coal bin, boss. Just an oil burner. He could hardly fit into *that*."

"So where is he?"

"Fortunately, X42 has been spared the humiliation which I must bravely bear alone. He was sent back to the shop last week for a slight readjustment."

"Lucky him. You hear anything from our copter or ground troops?"

"Not a whisper, chief. Are they coming?"

"They're supposed to."

"Oh, there'll be metal and bolts flying, limbs and torsos melting, wires exposed and shredded. It'll be horrid!"

"Horrid, eh? Tell me, just what was X42's problem?"

"Cowardice, boss. He developed a severe case of cowardice. Who would believe it?"

Suddenly it was getting very hot in the copter. I wiped my brow. "Stand by, X41."

I tried to raise the Security Plus copter. No dice. It was a bit early, but I tried the ground crew. No soap. I was too far away to reach the alarm board by talkie, and the communo was back in the car. But there were other ways to contact home base once I hit the plant.

"I'm coming down," I told X41.

"If you insist," the mech said. "But you'll have to find your own hiding place. There's only room in this closet for one, and I was here first."

CHAPTER 5

The copter took off behind me, Restly abandoning his scoop, and me too. Easy come, easy go. I couldn't see the damn thing because it was pitch dark, but I could hear it plain enough. I just hoped the boys in the plant weren't listening or I'd have more of a welcoming committee than a man of my modest temperament could stand.

I waited a while till the sound died away, then got moving.

A flash I'd borrowed from the Channel V news crew lit my way. I was in a small valley, about an eighth of a mile from the plant. Grass and trees were on either side of me. Odors of the countryside mingled with something that smelled vaguely like burnt rubber: Miklib making its presence felt. No moon peeked out from behind the clouds. An owl hooted somewhere. I could feel the weight of my laser in my pocket. Reassuring, all right. But not half as reassuring as if I'd been home in bed where I belonged and some other guy was doing this, someone less lovable and more expendable. I had the vague feeling that I wasn't really head of Security Plus, but one of its junior flunkies—some miserable clod they send out to risk his neck because all

the mechs got rusted during the last rainstorm, and the few
human ops were all on holiday.

Except "they" was me, and I could hardly find fault with
someone so me-like, could I?

I hoofed it uphill, wishing that Miklib had had the good
sense to install a mobile walk. No one got in my way. No
one started shooting. All that, I figured, would come later—
in about five minutes maybe. Definitely not later enough.

The plant was a dark patch against the lighter darkness
of the night. I rested for a moment, letting my breath catch
up with me. My eyes searched the sky, hunting for the
trusty Security Plus copter. Still nothing. I listened for the
sound of my faithful ground troops zooming over the terrain
for a last-minute rescue—namely mine. If there was one
thing we human ops tried to avoid, it was possible danger.
And this situation was full of it. More nothing. I used the
talkie on its long-distance frequency. All I got was a lot of
static. I beeped X41.

"Yes, boss?"

"Anything happening?"

"Not in the closet, chief. I couldn't tell you about the
rest of the plant."

"Thanks, X41. Next time there's a scrap-metal drive,
start sweating."

"Mechs don't sweat, skipper."

"Uh huh. Stand by for further instructions."

"Righto."

I moved forward. It was obvious that no one was going
to come to my rescue, except me. The me I'd tried to keep
out of harm's way these past four years by quitting the field
and assuming what should've been a nice restful desk job,
but almost never was. I wondered if I was still up to the
rough and tumble of fieldwork. There was only one way to
find out.

For all I knew, the robbery was over and done with and
the bad guys had already gone. It was a thought, all right,

the only cheerful one I'd managed to come up with in the last few minutes.

The front door of the Miklib Plant was locked tight. I made my way around the side of the building. The back door didn't budge either. I kept going. But not for long. A large hole in the wall greeted me, one big enough to drive a truck through. For all I knew, maybe someone had. What was wrong with these creeps, had they no sense of decorum?

I retraced my steps to the back door, fumbled in my pocket for the override cube, found it and overrode the magno locks. I got my laser out, doused the flash, took a deep breath, and pushed open the door.

No one was there. I dug an inspection cube out of my pocket, flashed it around the doorway. No spotter devices had been planted to unmask an intruder. As if the guys looting the place couldn't care less. Either they were very dumb, or figured they were invincible. It wasn't going to take me long to find out which.

I moved silently down a lightless hallway, letting the wall guide me. The inspection cube kept me posted on the various gadgets I passed: heating pipes, sprinkler system, dial-a-girlie video hot line, management spy peephole, loading tube, dial-another-girlie video hot line. Jeez.

Putting the cube on *seek*, I was led down a couple of more corridors, up a short staircase to the mezzanine, and from there to another locked door. The override cube did its work and I entered a small, musty, windowless room, about the size of a cell. Here was the Security Plus control outpost, what there was of it. All our systems were mech-installed and inspected, and no human noggin was big enough to carry around all the details. Mine carried none for this plant. But with good old Security Plus gear, I could find my way around the system anyway. I relocked the door from the inside, beat it over to the desk.

Fishing an operations cube out of my pocket, I thumbed the right dot. The desktop parted and up popped a miniature control board. I punched the home office button.

"Yes-s-s-s?" the alarm board intoned. "You rang?"

"Damn right I did. What's going on over here?"

"The Miklib Plant," the board informed me, "is in the process of being robbed."

"Still?"

"Alas, yes. They seem to be dismantling it piece by piece."

"How many of them are there?"

"Eight. There were ten, but two have already driven away with a truck full of spoils."

"Enterprising group."

"Most," the alarm board agreed.

"More than can be said for our side. Where the hell *is* everybody?"

"Well, *you* are there."

"So I am. This is hardly a one-man mission."

"There *is* X41."

"Yeah, in some closet. Quit stalling, pal, just tell me what's going on."

"Well, the troops started out."

"And?"

"You know Chief Constable Krimshaw?"

"Sure I know him. I just left the guy."

"Then you are, no doubt, aware that an arrest was made at the Truff Tool Works."

"So?"

"Well, he, dozens of newsmen, and hundreds of idle spectators left for the station house. Together. In one large clump, as it were."

"What's that got to do with us?" I demanded.

"There was something of a traffic jam."

"Was?"

"Is."

"Didn't clear up?" I was getting that old sinking sensation in my stomach, as if my rubber duck had sprung a fatal leak and was going down for the third and last time, along with me.

"If anything," the alarm board said, "it has become worse. Half of downtown is tied up."

"Half?"

"More perhaps."

"That's worse, all right. And our mechs?"

"Our mechs collided with the chief constable's car."

"The chief's, you say?"

"Head-first."

"Hmmmm," I said. "He okay?"

"He escaped bodily harm."

"That's something."

"But he was furious. It was entirely an accident," the alarm board said. "But things are in turmoil just now."

"No telling when our troops will get here, I suppose?"

"It would be mere speculation on my part to hazard a guess."

"But you're going to try anyway."

"If you insist. Not tonight."

"Not?"

"Precisely. It appears they are being held for irresponsible driving."

"Held? Mechs? How can they do that?"

"Chief Constable Krimshaw can do anything when it comes to holding people."

"Mechs aren't people."

"I left word at our counsel's office. He will inform the court of that fact in the morning."

"Leaving the copter. Why isn't *it* here? It got caught in the jam, too?"

"That hardly seems likely, now does it? No, the copter was subject to a malfunction."

"A malfunction?"

"The motor fell out."

"Jesus!"

"Shall I summon the constables now?"

"That's all we need."

"You are *intent* on being foolhardy?"

"Not if I can help it. But another bailout by the law will give us a permanent black eye."

"What shall I do?"

"Get our lawyers out of bed, have 'em do something now; Lord knows we pay them enough. Pry some mechs off guard duty wherever possible. Wake a human op. Have 'em all hustle down here on the double."

"There are only two vehicles available."

"Tell them to take taxies," I said. "What's happening here in the plant?"

"They are in the process of loading another truck."

"Through the loading tube?"

"Quite right. They are on the third floor. The truck is in the motor pool in the subbasement garage. It is two-thirds full at the moment. Seven of the men are working upstairs, one is down below with the truck."

"These crackers are in no rush?"

"Why should they be? They are unaware that their nefarious deed has been uncovered."

"They're that dumb?"

"Hardly dumb. Using a new process totally unknown to me, they managed to short all the electrical warning devices from outside, before entry. And substituted spurious images on the H.Q. monitor. Of course, they could not know that that immediately triggered our backup system, undoing all their efforts. This, however, would surely have been futile were it not for the shrewd and decisive action taken by our mech on the spot."

"X41?" I asked. "You're kidding."

"Who else? By skillfully concealing himself in the closet and thus avoiding detection, he aroused a false sense of security in the culprits, allowing you to appear on the scene and apprehend them."

"Yeah, I can hardly wait to see how I'm going to do that little thing. Tell me," I said, "how come monitors were never put in the field offices, so someone on the scene could see what's going on in the rest of the building?''

"Because you never ordered them."

"I knew there was a good reason," I said.

CHAPTER 6

I put the inspection cube back on *seek*, planted the laser in my hand as though it had taken root there, and went hunting.

The thing to remember when you're working your way over unfamiliar territory and there're lots of unfriendlies around is not to bump into walls, fall down stairs, or walk into objects that make noise. I didn't need a memory course to help me remember. What might happen if I forgot was enough to keep the old noodle ticking.

I gave the inspection cube its quarry, was directed to go down. I decided against using the main staircase, which was apt to become too public without much notice. I continued hunting. It took a while before I found a door that didn't lead to another door, or hallway, or closet, but to a narrow back staircase. I stood there listening, heard nothing, swapped flash for laser and went on down.

The basement was loaded with shipping crates, cartons of various sizes, spare factory parts, and other items that kept getting in my way. My jaunt ended over in a far corner in front of a closet door. Opening it, I shone my light inside.

"I'll come quietly," X41 said, its hands raised above its head. "Why make trouble? Just kidding, skipper. As you know, we mechanicals enjoy a good laugh as much as the next object. Ha, ha.''

"Ha, ha, yourself. Put your hands down,'' I said, ''and come out of there.''

"Is it safe?''

"Not especially, kid. But if you stay in the closet, I melt you down at the office.''

"Righto, boss!'' The mech stepped out gingerly. ''Let's go get them. After you, chief, I'll guard the rear.''

"Yeah, rear. Listen, X41, we haven't got much time. I've a plan.''

"Oh, dear, you're serious, aren't you? Plans, yet. Why, they're the worst of all. Someone's bound to get hurt.''

"Don't worry, chum, it probably won't be you.''

" 'Probably' is hardly reassuring.''

"It'll have to do,'' I told him. ''No one promised you a picnic when you signed on for this expedition.''

"Signed on?'' X41 said. ''You really *are* crazy, aren't you?''

I came through the doorway bent double, the laser in my hand. No one shot at me. I straightened up, took in my surroundings.

I was in a large hall.

The floor stretched like a small highway before me. There were workbenches, machines, all kinds of mechanical gadgets I couldn't name. It was dark, except at the very end of the aisle where seven guys were working away under a couple of neon lights. You had to hand it to 'em, they really *were* taking apart the damn plant.

I watched them unscrewing large and small pieces of thingamajigs, whatzises, and whatchamacallits from larger hunks of immobile machinery as though what they were doing was sane and reasonable activity. If the profit were big enough, some people would say it was. I wondered just what kind of profit these rubes were pulling down. They were working up a sweat, all right, but they didn't seem to be in a panic. There wasn't even a lookout.

The dismantled parts were being stuffed into crates, dumped in the loading tube, and shot down to the sub-basement. Bye-bye to the rest of these parts. Unless something happened soon. I figured it just might.

My talkie beeped. "All set, skipper."

"You sure?"

"We mechs are programmed to be sure."

"Just checking."

I wiped the sweat from my brow, aimed the laser over the heads of the work crew, zeroed in on the water-pipe that fed the sprinkler system, and cut loose with a blast. The pipe shattered. A sheet of water gushed out, drenching men and machines.

Before these lads had a chance to figure out the score and do something about it, X41 flicked on the juice.

The machines began to stir as electricity pulsed through them.

They didn't stir for long. Electricity and water made contact.

Sparks, lots of crackling, then something that looked like lightning. The floor shook with a small explosion. Black smoke poured out of the machines as though they had been magically turned into chimneys. A few screams were added to the tumult.

The lights shorted out, plunging the whole plant into darkness.

If the looters figured their troubles had reached a peak, they had another guess coming. Despite the shorting of the electrical system, the alarm siren kicked in. Only X41 at the controls of a backup system could explain it. But these birds didn't know beans about that.

There wasn't much to see here anymore, the show was over. I turned tail and beat it.

I took the stairs down two at a time. I wouldn't've minded riding the loading tube down, which was big enough for a bunch of Dunjers. But the tube was on the blink now, along with almost everything else in the joint. Except the alarm, which was still crooning away as if trying to win an audition. I hoped the racket would inspire my felons to do the right thing—take off in a hurry.

I hit the basement and kept going.

I slowed as I neared the subbasement, beeped X41.

"You in place?" I asked.

"Exposed is more like it. Subject to this madman's wrath should he lay eyes on me."

The "madman" was the truck loader.

"Where is he right now?"

"Still by the truck."

"Too close," I said.

"Surely you're not going to ask me to go ahead with this dreadful scheme, risking torso, wires, and bolts, are you?"

"X41," I said, "why don't you pretend for the next minute or two that you're *not* human, and do your job?"

"Not human?"

"Listen, X41, the guys from upstairs will be breathing down our necks any second."

"They will?"

"Come on, have a heart, pal."

"Surely you jest. As is well known—"

"They've got missile projectiles," I said. "Remember?"

The mech sighed. "Very well, chief, if you insist."

"Good old piece of junk," I murmured, wiping the sweat from my forehead.

I crept down the remaining few stairs, very slowly pushed open the door to the subbasement.

Pitch black inside.

I didn't let it worry me. Mech eye cells don't need any light. Infrared does the trick every time. I waited. The seconds crawled by like poisoned caterpillars. I was beginning to wonder if the old trooper had lost his nerve again, and just how that was possible in the first place, when a familiar voice from inside the basement called, "Yoo-hoo!"

I heard a curse, the sound of someone tripping.

"This way," X41 called.

A light flared. A burly guy was crouching behind a truck, next to the loading tube. He had a flash in one hand, a gun in the other. He was peering toward a row of trucks parked on the other side of the basement. A metal arm waved from between the trucks. The big guy fired but the arm was gone.

Leaving the truck, he moved in pursuit, his back to me. I could've plugged him, waited for his pals to show up, and, with some luck, picked 'em off one by one. Or without luck, been picked off by them. That second part gave me pause. That, and the thought of killing eight guys. I figured it might louse up my digestion. Not to mention the type of dreams I could expect for the next couple of years. Besides, I had bigger game in mind. My not having screwed up in this joint was making me ambitious. Or reckless. I wasn't sure which yet.

I stepped through the doorway, silently tiptoed toward the truck. With the siren going full blast, I could've fallen flat on my face and the guy wouldn't've heard me. He was out of sight now, playing hide-and-seek with my mech.

I gave X41 a mental tip of the hat, hoisted myself onto the back of the truck.

My pal with the gun had only done a so-so job of packing. But then he hadn't been hired for neatness. I buried myself behind a pile of crates, pulled a tarpaulin over me, and beeped the mech.

"Still among the living?"

"Just barely."

"Okay, I'm fixed for the duration. Lose him."

"Aye aye, skipper."

"I'll see you get a hero medal for this, X41."

"I'd rather have stayed in the closet."

I lay still listening to my own breathing. There was no reason for these turkeys to think I was in here. If I didn't cough, sneeze, or break into song, I was all right, depending on how you defined "all right." Taking risks like this wasn't in my line anymore. But the company needed a boost just about now, and this looked like an okay way to get one. It would look swell on my resumé, if I lived long enough to add it.

"He's still hunting for me, boss," my talkie said.

"Where are you?"

"In an empty oil drum."

"He going to find you?"

"When it comes to oil drums, I know how to pick them. Far off in a corner."

"Should be safe enough even for you, eh, X41?"

"Guarding this plant was supposed to be safe, and look what happened."

"It's the nature of the job," I said.

"Now he tells me."

CHAPTER 7

I lay under the tarpaulin cradling my laser like a long-lost lover. The truck rumbled along on the highway. Every once in a while I craned my neck, peered through a crack in the sideboards. No multilevel expressways were in sight. No lights twinkled from giant skyscrapers. There weren't even any slum sections handy to give me that special down-at-home feeling. It was dark outside, but occasional head-lights gave me a clue to my whereabouts. We were heading away from Happy City, were somewhere on a cross-country road, a no-man's-land between the city-states. Brigands, pirates, and highwaymen ran the show here, had a field day heisting hapless travelers. But since they'd already got me, why worry? Especially if they didn't know it. What I *did* have to worry about was our destination. Leaving Happy City hadn't been part of my plan.

Two guys were in the truck's cabin. Another truck was keeping us company, this one empty of stolen property, I hoped, and containing only what was left of the bad guys. For all I knew, we were bound for some out-of-the-way hospital where they could get themselves patched up. I figured there had to be some injuries considering what I'd done to 'em.

I wondered who these creeps were. Guys in the scrap metal business? It seemed like a tough way to get hold of lots of useless junk. Maybe these were Miklib competitors trying to sink their rival? That almost made sense, though a well-planted bomb would've done a helluva lot more damage.

The motor, meanwhile, purred under me like a tipsy tiger. The bumps in the road made me bounce around like a Ping-Pong ball. Talk about earning my fee! I squinted through the peephole again. We were still heading in the wrong direction.

The city-states didn't get along with each other no-how. Didn't these crackers know that? When you left your own city-state you took your life in your hands. In fact, in most city-states you were in trouble even if you *did* belong there. Trouble City was a good example. But it was peachy next to the really *bad* places.

Deep Hate Junction, Mobsville, Strangleburg, Fearsville, Fearsburg, and No-Chance Township were all places it was better to read about than visit. They made Happy City seem like a paradise by comparison. And Happy City was no great shakes.

Long ago, most citizens worked under the old Federal Government. When it went broke, *everyone* went to the cleaners. Naturally, people took it personally. Personal Grudge City came into existence right around then. And that was it for the Feds. Curtains. A lot of no-trespass signs went up, and plenty of moats, walls, and drawbridges. Ack-ack blasted neighbors' planes out of the sky till some treaties were signed. And those hardly helped at all. Smilesville, Friendship Haven, and Loveburg are only a bit better than their tougher rivals. For all I knew, folks might like nothing better than to change back to the old rotten system and go broke all over again. Only no one's asked them lately.

When the truck began to slow I returned my eye to the crack and took another look-see. We were approaching some kind of roadblock. Great. The last thing I needed was to be hijacked by *strangers*, crooks Security Plus hadn't even been hired to guard against. The Detective's Handbook said nothing about *that*. I just hoped *my* crooks could still put up a fight. The thought of having to lend 'em a hand was a real hoot.

I looked again. And whatever smidgen of cheer I had left went by the boards.

These weren't bandits. By comparison bandits were friendly, playful types. What I was eyeballing here were half a dozen grim-faced guys in coarse gray uniforms, black cartridge belts, military caps, rifles, tommy guns, and a bazooka. If I ever wanted to start a small war, I'd know where to come. These birds were ready for one.

I recognized the uniforms, all right. We were being halted by border guards from Fearsburg. Fearsburg, of all places! When my crooks could've chosen a *nice* city-state like Lost Cause City, Scavengerburg, or No Hope Juncture, where they at least gave you a square meal before they shot you. I wanted to crawl out and warn them, tell 'em to turn back. But it was already too late. We'd come to a halt. Two of the guards were lumbering over while the rest of them stood around fingering their guns, as if assuring the weapons they'd be in use any moment.

A small still voice in my noggin said, "Mommy," while another cried, "Hide under the floorboards, quick!" What I needed was a jet out of there, not dumb voices in the bean. Any second I expected to hear the inevitable gunshots. I figured I could stand that. The part that came after, during the search, where I hold off all of Fearsburg with my laser, that was the part I could've done without.

The truck started up again with a jerk, sent me spilling. I got my eye to the crack in time to see the guards saluting as we drove away.

Saluting?

I sank back against the floor, not sure whether to congratulate myself or say my final prayers. There'd long been a lot of idle chitchat in Happy City about which was worse,

Fearsville or Fearsburg. It looked as if I was going to find out at least part of the answer.

We hit two more checkpoints before we reached the city proper. I kept my eye glued to the crack. The only folks out on the streets were the cops. They had on black uniforms, walked in pairs, and looked just about as sweet-tempered as the border guards.

No cars drove by, except those with nice police insignias on their sides.

Houses were short, squat, and dark.

The only lights came from dim street lamps and neon signs. One showed a giant ear. The caption read: LOOSE TALK KILLS. Another pictured a huge eye. WATCH YOUR NEIGHBOR. A third simply said OBEY. It flashed on and off in the empty street as if daring someone to disagree. There were no takers. Everyone was hiding out indoors. Except us, of course. We seemed to be getting the royal treatment. The only non-cops to be prowling around. Well, I knew *I* wasn't a cop in Fearsburg. But could I make the same admirable statement about the rest of this crew? Who the hell had I hitched a ride with?

If nothing else, I'd learned one small thing: why they called this Fearsburg. I'd only been here a few minutes and already I was afraid.

We drove a while longer. None of the inspiring sights outside my peephole changed much. Fearsburg didn't build big. Their modest ambitions might have seemed dandy somewhere else, but in this hamlet the big expenditures probably went for handcuffs and billy clubs.

Downtown wasn't much different from the sticks. Only one tall building was set aside in a large vacant square. Either town hall, or a prison. Just looking at the joint made me want to confess. It was the one place I didn't want to end up in. Naturally, that's where we headed.

We swung around to the rear, wide doors opened, a ramp led down, and we went with it.

My peephole revealed a cavernous, ill-lit, underground garage. We cruised to a stop. I heard the guys in the cabin climb out.

This was the ticklish part, all right.

If these lugs decided to unload now, one of the things they'd be unloading was *me*. Odds were, they wouldn't like it. I wasn't worth half as much as the dumb junk they'd copped, and they'd probably resent the fact.

Back home, if push had come to shove, I could've plugged 'em with impunity almost. But here *I* was the interloper, the guy with no rights. The notion took some getting used to.

I lay there under my tarpaulin, my fingers around the laser as if hand and gun had been welded together. I was sweating so much the tarpaulin would start to leak any second.

Expecting the worst, it took me a moment to realize nothing bad was happening. Yet.

I turned my eye to the crack again. That stupid crack and I had become bosom buddies, all but inseparable. Outside were a few parked vehicles and lots of empty space. The goon squad had decamped, gone off to file its report, or tend to its wounds. I was alive and well in Fearsburg, if that wasn't a contradiction in terms.

So far, alive and well.

The only guys in the streets were cops. And the only cars belonged to them. I'd never make it out of town on foot anyway. But a squad car was a possibility.

Or a truck.

No one had bothered the trucks coming here. So why couldn't I leave the same way?

I rose very slowly, cautiously, as if I'd just had a head transplant and wasn't sure the new item would stay in place. No one ran over to grab me. I dug my flash out and daintily made my way around and over all the Miklib stuff, until I reached the truck's rear. Parting the canvas, I peeked out. All clear. I put one foot over the side, then the other, and lowered myself to the ground.

I had hitched my ride here to get the lowdown on the crooks, to find out who they worked for and what they were up to. Simple, praiseworthy objectives. But "here" had turned out to be Fearsburg, and the only way to nab the baddies would be to start a war. There hadn't been one of those in ages. None of the city-states had the resources for a bloody, full-fledged war. Or even the ambition. Not when home turf was still ripe for picking.

So if I put my neck on the line and poked around here, what good would it do me? None at all. Thirty years on the job had honed my sleuthing skills to a sharp edge. But the thought of getting out alive was even more compelling. Back in Happy City I'd report to Mayor Strapper and let him handle it. Maybe he'd write a note of protest.

A quick inspection of the other vehicles told me that none of them were squad cars. That left the truck. Lord knows what made it special. I just hoped it was.

I didn't think my driver had thoughtfully left the key in the ignition, but I had a couple of cubes that might do the trick. If not I could always rig the wires. I started for the cabin.

A booming voice barked: "WELCOME, DUNJER! WELCOME!"

CHAPTER **8**

Bright lights flared, blinding me momentarily. I put up a palm, shielded my eyes.

"It has been a long time, sir," the same voice said minus the irritating amplification. That voice sounded suspiciously familiar.

I squinted into the bright light and saw him. Instantly, I closed my eyes. But the rotten sight wouldn't go away. I'd been right all along: this really *wasn't* my day.

He was a large, stout party, dressed in black slacks, a white dinner jacket, and black bow tie. His round head was completely bald. His nose was ample, eyebrows bushy, lips full and pouting. Peering through half-closed lids I saw him start toward me. He waddled as he walked, as if some prankster seal had donned a human costume. Three chins jiggled with each step he took. His protruding belly joined in the fun.

"My dear sir, I cannot tell you what a great pleasure this is. To meet in such an unexpected manner, and here, no less, in this delightful city-state, so noted for its quaint charm and hospitality. How marvelously fitting."

He grabbed my hand and pumped it up and down as though I were a slot machine he wanted to test.

The thing to do, obviously, was kill him and get the hell out of there in a hurry. But like a lot of good ideas, this one was a bit ahead of its time.

My fat pal wasn't quite alone. We had plenty of company giving us the eye. The last time I'd gotten this much attention, I was being audited by the Happy City Tax Board.

Guys in black uniforms were at both ends of the garage blocking any and all exits, about three dozen of 'em. They weren't the Fearsburg Men's Chorus either. Each gripped some kind of gun. They had enough firepower between them to level a small army. Only there wasn't any army—just me. It could've been me because of my tough, no-holds-barred fighting spirit. But right now I seemed to've mislaid it.

"Dr. Spelville," I said, my voice sounding squeaky and high-pitched as though I were trying to mimic some push-over these birds wouldn't want to touch with a ten-foot pole. Let alone shoot.

"Indeed, yes." The doctor grinned. "How generous of you to remember. In a world such as ours, the gracious gesture is so rare."

I nodded at the mean-looking gunmen. "Called the troops out, I see. Well, they sure got an eyeful; rare gestures like this shouldn't be missed. Can I go now?"

He smiled at me. "In due time, sir. Perhaps."

"You're not sure?"

"Mr. Dunjer, you should consider your reception here an honor, and enjoy it—while it lasts."

"Deep humility has always made me forego honors."

"You always did have a delicious sense of humor." Spelville chuckled. "Let me tell you, sir, as soon as the monitors revealed that we had an unexpected guest, and that it was, of all people, *you*, I immediately summoned an honor guard on your behalf." He lowered his voice. "We do go back a long way; Mr. Dunjer, do we not?"

"Uh huh."

The last time I'd tangled with this fat bird, he'd been

running a nuthouse on the outskirts of Happy City. There'd been a minor fracas, and one of the inmates they kept around just for such purposes tried to rip me limb from limb. On another occasion, the good doctor had attempted to blow me up. There hadn't been a third occasion till now, so I was still alive and kicking. For the moment, anyway.

"They don't smile," I said.

"The security forces?"

"Yeah. I thought they were just cops."

"It is the same thing here, you know."

"I hadn't known."

"Oh, yes. But security forces have so much *more* authority, wouldn't you say? Why, they can do absolutely *anything* they wish." He looked around. "Come to think of it, I never *have* seen them smile. And I've been here for two solid years. Yes, Mr. Dunjer, right here in City Hall."

"Place looks like a prison," I complained.

"Why, it's that, too, of course. As well as a great many other things. Our little town is noted for its sense of economy."

"I'm sure. Just what is it you do here, Spelville?"

"I, sir, am Commissioner of Intercity Trade."

"Congratulations. I didn't know there was any."

"But of course. Why, the truck you arrived on was engaged in that very thing."

"That truck was full of stolen goods."

"Goodness, our entrepreneurs are even more enterprising than I imagined." He beamed at me. "How simply marvelous."

The room was up on the ninth floor, almost a tower in this neck of the woods. It seemed to be comfortable enough, like some high-class hotel that was a bit run-down at the heels. The bed was ornate with a canopy. The carpet was thick enough to tickle my ankles. The armchairs were doubly padded. The large framed mirror on the wall would let me see the Dunjer I'd grown up with and trusted, even if he had gotten me into this pickle. The one thing missing was the view—there wasn't any. Someone had forgotten to put in the windows.

"Yes," Dr. Spelville said, "all the comforts of home."

I nodded. This was the perfect time to wring the fat doctor's neck. We were alone. Almost. Except for the pair of mechs on either side of the door, who looked as keen and observant as dime-store Indians. They hadn't moved an inch since we'd entered the room, which, unfortunately, didn't mean they couldn't. I decided to put off wringing my host's neck for a while. It seemed the smart thing to do.

The doctor waddled over to a door, flung it open. "Look here," he said, as if about to unveil hidden treasure.

I waded through the carpet, took a peek at the bathroom. No windows there either. But a pair of long bath towels hung on a marble rack. Both bore the inscription WELCOME DUNJER.

"Certainly makes a man feel wanted," I said.

"As it was meant to, sir." Spelville rubbed his hands together, winked at me, all but went into a jig.

"Of course," I said, "you had no idea I was coming."

He shrugged. "How could I? Your presence here among us was a *total* surprise. But we in Fearsburg have learned to move with alacrity. Hospitality is our byword, you know."

"News to me, pal."

The rotund medic nodded thoughtfully. "Bad press. Other, less hospitable city-states envy us. You have no idea, sir."

"Name doesn't help much either, I bet."

"Ah, there you have it. I cannot tell you how often I have discussed this matter with the City Fathers. I have submitted numerous suggestions, as you might well imagine. I felt it my patriotic duty to do so: Sweetburg, Blissful Corner, More-Than-Plentyville, Love Nest, even—surely in some ways the most apt of all. But to no avail. Something about tradition. The City Fathers, I fear, are determined to retain 'Fearsburg' at all costs.''

"I heard there was just one father," I told him.

"The General, you mean. A common misconception. I cannot begin to understand how these silly stories gain such currency. The General, of course, is a father himself." Spelville held up a stubby finger. "That makes one. Then there is the General's father. Which makes two. The General's mother also has a father; in short, the *grandfather*. And while he is a bit infirm these days, even decrepit, some have said, his mind on good days is razor-sharp."

"He has good days, eh?"

"Assuredly. He had one four months ago. So you see, Mr. Dunjer, *three* City Fathers. Refuting once and for all the base canard which our more envious neighbors have seen fit to circulate."

"And this is really City Hall?"

"Absolutely. And, as I pointed out, the city prison. As well as the Bureau of Taxation, Ministry of Positive Information—one can never be positive enough, can one?—the Grand Justice of Final Appeals, that's the General again, and the General's Own Retail Clothing Mart. Not to mention the General's Kiddy Toy Shop, Shopping Emporium, and Cut-Rate Hardware Outlet."

"People buy that stuff?"

"They wouldn't dare not to. Fearsburg, you know."

"Uh huh."

"Also, the Intercity Trade Commission."

"Namely you."

"A man must make a living. After you so injudiciously curtailed my ministry to those poor misfits, the mentally deranged in Happy City, what was I to do? I had no choice but to look elsewhere. Fortunately there was an opening right here in this most pleasant city-state for a man of my rather special talents."

"Yeah, special. Like shanghaiing me to this rotten burg." The doctor drew himself up tall. "That, sir, is a very *negative* thing to say. We do not appreciate negativity here in Fearsburg. Was it *my* fault, Mr. Dunjer, that you chose to stow away on one of our Intercity Trade trucks?''

"This some kind of a nutty pinch, Spelville?" I asked.

"My dear sir, trade is my game, not law enforcement."

"Game, eh?"

"Precisely, Mr. Dunjer, and I am delighted that you have come to play with us. Simply delighted."

I was alone again. A great time to take it easy, think things out, or maybe just cut my throat. I hadn't decided which yet, but I was leaning toward the latter.

The fat worm had taken my talkie, all my cubes, and my laser. He'd've taken my socks, too, if they'd seemed important. But one thing Fatso could never take, and that was my dignity—mostly because it was already shot to hell.

Whadda mess!

The word "sucker" flashed on and off in my noodle like a shorted light bulb. Just what I needed in this muddle, light bulbs on the brain. For a second I saw myself in a cop's uniform directing traffic on one of Happy City's worst intersections—the one the natives dubbed Death's Highway, mostly because of the eight intersecting speed lanes, but also because the traffic light was always on the blink.

Of course, it'd never come to that. I had a couple of options, things I could do if worse came to worst. Like dusting off my private-eye shingle. I could go snooping after errant spouses and missing house pets again. Or if that didn't pan out, maybe get a job with Krimshaw as assistant to the office boy—the one that's on permanent latrine duty.

The word "screwup" took the place of "sucker," not much of an improvement. The problem was simple enough, even simpleminded: the president of Security Plus was supposed to be a real wiz, a guy too sharp to be laid low by the enemy. That's what our ads all said, and the guys who wrote 'em made more than I did. The board of directors and stockholders probably felt the same way. Why not?

They were part of the public, and our ad boys had been flimflamming the public for years. When I got back to the old home base, I could expect a ton of woe if word of my foul-up leaked out. And why shouldn't it?

Provided I ever got back—a big proviso, all right. The trouble with landing in Fearsburg was that when one lunatic—like Spelville—got done with you, there were a dozen others waiting to take a crack at you. The town, along with its dumb General, was strictly wacko. There were stories of hapless travelers who got gummed up in this burg and ended up in cans of cat food. I liked cats, but I wasn't a fanatic about it.

I sighed, took off my coat and jacket, loosened my tie, removed my shoes, and stretched out on the bed. The place was probably full of spotter eyes, catcher ears, and Lord knows what else. I certainly didn't, not without my usual arsenal of cubes. It hardly mattered. Let 'em watch and listen, as if I were some Tri-D special. There wasn't much I could do that Spelville'd find entertaining.

The whole thing at Miklib had been a setup, its main aim to get me here, though I couldn't rule out that the theft of machinery hadn't been a motive too. Plainly, Spelville had a pretty good idea of how my outfit operated, and what it'd take to snare me. What he didn't know, the one important fact he'd overlooked, was that for a reasonable fee, I made personal appearances. I'd've been only too glad to turn up in Fearsburg and give my noted anticrime lecture, without all this fuss.

Somehow, I doubted that's what the fat jerk had on his mind.

So what *was* on his mind?

Revenge?

I hardly rated it. The fracas in Happy City had been small potatoes. And he'd tried to blow *me* up, not the other way around, a trivial but not totally unimportant point. Two years was a long time, too. And dragging me out all the way to

Fearsburg was doing it the hard way. I could've been way-laid more easily right at the plant.

One thing was pretty certain. Whatever the crumb was up to, I wasn't going to like it. I'd only been here a short while and already I hated it.

Spelville had generously left me my watch. It was twelve-thirty. I twisted the watch around on my wrist, unlatched the back, activated the homing device, and returned it to the right direction. Unless the spotter eye was planted directly over my head—always a possibility—my move had escaped detection.

I folded my arms in back of my head and closed my eyes. Staying awake and worrying about this mess would only give me a headache. And I had that already. A little shut-eye would be just the ticket.

I'd barely dozed off when a knock sounded on the door.

At least they were being polite.

"Yeah," I called, "come in."

The door opened.

"Step on it, boss, let's blow before they wise up."

It was X41.

CHAPTER 9

I sat up, eyeing the clanky contraption as if waiting for it to burst into song, or dance, or more likely, vanish in a puff of smoke, while the next act took over—Spelville doing magic tricks. I was either having a theatrical nightmare, or had gone off my rocker. The alarm board, I knew, immobile as it was and plugged firmly into the wall, might somehow find a way to get here in a pinch. But not X41. His self-preservation instincts were even better developed than mine.

"You were expecting Miss Happy City maybe? Come on, boss, stop staring. Let's not press our luck; you can admire me back at the office."

"You're real?"

"Is this the beginning of a philosophical discussion?" it asked suspiciously.

"And you made a joke?"

"I said I could."

"Yeah, so you did. And since there're no alarms chiming, or armed guards rushing in here to beat us to a pulp, I guess you also took care of all the other stuff too, like the devices planted in this room."

"At their source. The main control room."

"Did everything," I said in some wonder. "You press pants on the side, too?"

"Honestly, skipper, I think we should let my one joke suffice and get out of here."

"Uh huh." The old tub of wires was right. I leaned over, began lacing my shoes. "How'd you find this room?" I asked.

"The homing device."

"Glad I did *something* right. You tailed me here?"

"What else could I do?"

"File a missing person report?"

"The faithful mech was not about to desert the chief in his hour of need."

"He wasn't?"

"Tossing caution to the wind, I jumped into one of the Miklib vehicles and gave hot pursuit. Oh, it was touch and go for a while, skipper. Especially at the checkpoints."

I stood up. "What'd you do?"

"I told them I was with the two trucks ahead."

"And they bought it?"

"Why not? We were all driving Miklib trucks. It wasn't unreasonable to believe that the guards would think me part of the convoy and wave me through. I was willing and eager to take the chance."

I peered at the mech. "You feeling all right?"

"I am in fine fettle, thank you. And yourself?"

"In shock. But don't worry, I'll get over it in a few years."

"We'll all be rooting for you, boss."

I went through the door. Both of the mechs that had been guarding me were stretched out in the hall. A cheering sight. They looked as inert as thumbtacks, but not half as useful.

"Follow me, boss."

We started hiking. The hallway at this hour was empty. I didn't mind. I'd had enough fun for one night.

I glanced back at the fallen hardware.

"I see your scramblers are still up to par," I said.

"I counted on that, chief. But it takes nerves of steel."

"Computer chips, in your case."

That our scramblers were superior didn't surprise me any, they were supposed to be. All security mechs came equipped with built-in scramblers and scrambler defenses. What scramblers did was scramble other mechs' innards and make 'em fall down. How long they stayed down depended on how hard they'd been hit and the quality of their antiscramblers to undo the damage. Sometimes it took minutes, other times, hours. And there'd been occasions when mechs ended up back at the factory for fine retooling.

Our Security Plus product packed a king-sized wallop; that was expected. What wasn't was X41's behavior. I'd've fed our other mechs what he'd been imbibing, except mechs don't imbibe.

"We'd better use the staircase, capn. Even at one-ten the lift may be occupied."

"Back stairs," I said. "Always the *back* stairs when on a hush-hush job."

"I've read the Detective's Handbook, too," the mech told me. "The back stairs are right through this doorway."

"Good thinking, X41."

We started down.

"You didn't run across Spelville's hangout, by any chance?" I asked.

"If you mean the fat gentleman in the white jacket, yes. I was hidden down the hall when he and the guards took you up in the lift. It would have been foolish to follow. I therefore decided to wait till you activated the homing device before beginning my rescue mission. Meanwhile, I reconnoitered, searching for the main control room."

"Manned by mechs?"

" 'Manned' is hardly the right word, chief. 'Operated' would be far more accurate. It was operated by only one mechanical in this case. I scrambled him. Then I disarmed the alarm system and blanked out parts of the various surveillance devices."

"Couldn't've done better myself," I said.

"With all due modesty, boss, probably not half as well. Spotter eyes are in all the hallways. I spied the fat gentleman entering an office on the sixth floor. He was there only a moment, then left again."

"He carrying anything?"

The mech nodded. "On his way in. One laser, one talkie, a number of cubes, a wallet, a flashlight marked 'Property of Channel V News Copter—thieves will be prosecuted,' and two tickets to the Annual Happy City Girlie Show. He left empty-handed."

"Let's drop down there," I said.

"Must we?"

"Yeah. Those tickets cost a fortune."

"I suppose there's no way I can persuade you to leave well enough alone?"

"Now *that's* the X41 I know," I said cheerfully.

The door to Spelville's office wasn't locked. The mech and I breezed right in. I marched over to his desk, flicked on the lamp.

"You dampen the alarms here?" I asked.

"Of course. The possibility that you might do something reckless *did* occur to me."

"You doped it out right, pal."

I pulled open the top drawer. The former contents of my pockets lay there in a neat pile, looking neglected. I began returning all the items to their rightful place.

"You talk a good strategy, X41," I said. "But there's more to the security game than playing it safe. There's risk-taking galore, constant exposure to danger, the perilous infiltration of enemy strongholds."

"You mean all the things I've just done?"

I sighed. "Yeah, precisely."

I went over to an olive drab filing cabinet by the wall, tried it. Locked. I used my override cube. When that didn't work, I fried the lock with a laser blast and swung open the door.

"If we ever get back to Happy City," I told the mech, "I'll see you get promoted to president, while I go off on permanent vacation. How's that?"

"Hardly necessary, chief, I'll settle for a simpler reward."

"Chairman of the board?"

I began ruffling through files. There weren't all that many. The darn things *were* trade agreements with nearby city-states. They seemed legitimate enough, as far as I could tell, which wasn't all that far, really.

"Permanent office cleanup duty, perhaps," X41 said.

"Sorry, kid. We've got a waiting list a mile long for that spot," I told him. "For chairman there's almost no competition at all. Who wants the hot seat? Post's almost as bad as being president."

I looked under H for Happy City. I half-expected to run across records titled *Miklib Plant Robbery*. There was a file labeled *Happy City*, all right, but it was empty. As if it had been cleaned out.

"Boss," X41 said, "if we stay here much longer, they'll think we belong and give us work details."

"One second," I said. I returned to the desk, went through the rest of the drawers.

"Plenty of office supplies," I said, "but not much else. For a guy in charge of intercity trade, Spelville was kind of skimpy with the paperwork."

"Why not, chief? If the trade was mostly hijacked and stolen goods, records would be the last thing he'd want to keep."

"Maybe. I can't see the General complaining, though. The whole thing was probably his idea anyway. He'd want to know that our fat friend was doing his job, bringing home the bacon. He might even value written reports, as evidence that he and Fearsburg were living up to their rotten reputation."

I went back to the filing cabinet, ran my fingers over a couple of well-chosen spots. "Hmmmm," I said.

"I think I'm starting to perspire," X41 said. "I honestly do. We must return to Happy City at once to document this miracle."

"Look," I said. "When I ran my finger over the inside wall of the cabinet, dust accumulated on it. But when I ran my finger over the empty Happy City space, it came out clean. What does that tell you?"

"That you've become hopelessly insane, boss."

"Uh uh, something more ominous. What it means is that Spelville recently, maybe even tonight, made off with the Happy City files. And why, you ask?"

"I didn't ask!"

"Because he knew we'd be here."

"He knew?"

I nodded. "The guy anticipated our every move."

"Then this is a trap!"

"Maybe not."

"No maybes about it, skipper. The logic of your thinking is inescapable. I'm doomed!"

"Something's goofy," I said. "But I can't figure out just what."

"Who could believe it?" X41 said. "*You* they'll only enslave. *Me*, they'll melt down and recast as a water pipe or something."

"Enslave, eh? Okay, you've got my attention. Let's vamoose, pal."

"Imagine, going through life as a water pipe."

I flicked off the desk lamp. "C'mon, let's beat it, X41."

"Beat it? Haven't you had enough violence for one day?"

"Go, stupid, it's time to go! What's the matter with you? I thought you *wanted* to go?"

"Go? Oh, *go!* Why didn't you say so? Of course I want to go."

I looked at my metal companion. "You're not really petrified with fear, are you?"

"Mechanicals are not built that way."

"So what's the story?"

"We have our little secrets too," the mech told me.

We were on the staircase, somewhere between the third and second floor, when the siren went off. It sounded like a fire drill in grade school, only a lot more noisy.

"Thought you'd fixed that," I said.

"So did I."

"This is no place to hang out," I said. "It's a potential bottleneck."

"Are you about to exercise your vaunted leadership qualities," X41 asked, "or shall I lead the way?"

"Come on."

We stepped out on the second floor. And almost collided with one of the black-clad troopers. He reached for his laser. Mine was already in my hand. I whacked him across the noodle. He went down like a telegraph pole struck by lightning.

"Left," I said.

We ran left.

Behind us the sound of lots of other running feet could be heard. We turned a corner. The siren was still screaming away. A bunch of mechs appeared down the hall.

"Too many for me to handle, skipper."

"That makes two of us."

Time to take cover. I stopped by a door. The knob wouldn't turn. I was all set to blast it with the laser when a half dozen troopers charged out of a side corridor a dozen feet away. I was busy considering whether to go down in a stupid blaze of glory, or do the sensible thing and give up, when they ran right by us without even a sideways glance.

"Fame's fleeting, all right," I said. "An hour ago they would've shot me for sure. Or at least clubbed me."

The mechs ran by us too. I was starting to feel nostalgic

for the good old times, like a few hours back, when people and objects paid attention to me.

The mechs got to the end of the hallway. They didn't quite make the turn. They began skidding and clanging around like a collection of tin cans held together by loose string.

"You doing that?" I asked.

"I would if I knew how, skipper. Even if they *are* part of the great mechanical brotherhood. The good of the cause, you know. But there're far too many of them."

One by one the mechs began to fall down. Some of them lay there twitching, others were as inert as wrenches or screwdrivers. I could hear firing going on outside.

Behind the locked office door I heard a loud, crashing sound, as if the outside wall had tumbled into the room in a valiant attempt to escape the cold night air.

The door burst open.

"Hi there, chief," XX21 said.

A flock of Security Plus mechs poured out into the hall, took up defensive positions around me. Shooting mechs whose specialty was shooting things, human or otherwise, depending on the circumstances. Super-scrambler mechs whose main function was the scrambling of their blood brothers, namely other mechs, computers, and anything else that looked menacing and wasn't halfway human. Spy mechs who could intercept talkie signals, telephone chatter, and the movement of mechs half a block away, not to mention the latest racetrack results hot off the wire. There was even Duffy, a short, pudgy, human op, in a rumpled three-piece suit and bowler hat. His eyes were bloodshot and he needed a shave. But what guy wouldn't at one-thirty A.M.?

"You couldn't've picked a better time to get caught?" Duffy complained.

Behind him I could see that the outer wall *was* gone. A dozen copters were bobbing in the night sky. Two were still unloading mechs into the office. More mechs, having donned suction cups, were climbing up the building's side, filling the office, too. Down below, the shooting had stopped.

"Almost looks like the whole firm's here," I said.

"It *is* here," Duffy said. "The mobile part anyway."

"Thought most of 'em were in the lockup."

"They were. I wasn't the only one the alarm board got outta bed."

"Roused our lawyers, eh?"

"Sure. And they woke a judge."

"Used the old habeas corpus, I bet."

"What habeas corpus? These aren't *people*, they're mechs. Judge threw the case outta court."

"Where'd we get the copters?"

"Rented them," Duffy said, "from Rent-A-Copter."

"Figures," I said.

Duffy sighed. "Used up the whole secret operations fund for the next three decades. No more free booze at Louie's."

"Boss," XX21 said, "we've got a copter hovering right outside."

"Yeah, time to go, gang." I started into the wall-less room, ready to flag down a copter.

"Unless you want to take over this city-state," XX21 said.

That stopped me in my tracks.

"Sure," Duffy said. "Our boys cornered some old guy in a uniform downstairs. Chest full of medals, white handlebar mustache, long sword, pistol, kid gloves, and riding boots. Says he's the General. Says if we spare his life, he'll give us Fearsburg."

"Any takers?" I asked the crowd around me. "No, eh? Tell the General we'll spare his life *this* time, but not to go messing around in Happy City again."

"We already told him the last part, boss," XX21 said. "He said he had nothing to do with it."

"Nothing?"

"They all say that," Duffy said.

"Yeah," I said. "And every once in a while, they're even telling the truth."

A squad of our mechs marched by. Cleanup operation. We got a salute. There was nothing left to clean up in the hall, so they went on their way.

"Listen, Duffy," I said, "the General had to know that Security Plus wouldn't stand for my being hijacked. He's got enough trouble keeping his people in line without a small-scale war on his hands."

"So what does it mean?" X41 asked. "It must mean *something*."

"Tell me," I asked XX21, "you airborne mechs get sprung before the alarm board pulled our other mechs off their posts, or after?"

"After."

"So there were two groups headed here?"

"Right. The first in cars."

"Rent-A-Ride?" Duffy asked.

The mech nodded.

"There goes our annual picnic," Duffy said. "Along with our New Year's party, and gifts to the needy—namely *us*. This *is* a black day, Dunjer!"

"The first group," XX21 said, "was radioed that the second group was on its way. It pulled up so both groups could meet and attack in unison."

"Smart tactics," I said. "Unless I was being drawn and quartered. Then you would've been too late."

"But we weren't too late," XX21 said. "We took precautions."

"Yeah?"

"Of course. When X41 called in from the plant after you rode off with the thieves—"

"I could do no less, chief," X41 said.

"—the alarm board instructed him to take after you."

"I'd have done it anyway," X41 said. "We mechs are almost fearless."

"He was told the rest of us would be at his heels, but our timetable was a bit off."

"I could have been *killed!*" X41 shouted.

"Some hero. With a whole army at his back," I said. "So who's left in Happy City minding the store?"

"Almost no one," XX21 said.

"Don't sweat it, capn," X41 said. "We'd've heard if there was trouble."

"How?"

"True, the talkies don't reach this far."

"And the Rent-A-Things," I said, "don't have communos."

Duffy put his arm around my shoulder. "Let me put your mind at rest, Tom. As the human op on the scene, I can assure you that things were *very* peaceful when we left Happy City."

"That was then," I pointed out. "What about now?"

"Now?"

"Yes," the alarm board said, "very hectic. All in all, I would say about eight break-ins have occurred during the last hour."

"Eight?" I said.

"More perhaps."

"More?"

"Who can say? Tapping constable lines is chancy at best. Especially since they learned we were intercepting their calls. They keep changing frequencies."

"Tricky bastards," Duffy said.

The alarm board said, "Only five of these sites were guarded by us. I use the term 'guarded' advisedly, since two of the sites had no mechanicals at all on the premises, once we pulled our contingent—merely alarm systems, and the others only skeletal staffs. That is, one mechanical apiece. Naturally, they could offer only token resistance before they were neutralized."

"The alarms at least go off?"

"No, but the backup systems did. Unfortunately, we had no reserves to send in response."

"What was Krimshaw up to in all this?" I asked.

"Run ragged. His men were stretched rather thin for a wholesale assault on the city."

"And the other agencies?"

"Attempting to cope. Should I tap their lines?"

"Don't bother," I said. "We can read about it in the papers. Everything quiet now?"

"Certainly. What's left to steal?"

"Okay," I told the alarm board. "Sit tight."

"I was hardly planning to gallivant around town. Even if I could."

"Yeah. Over and out."

I exchanged glances with the rest of the gang packed into the small Fearsburg communications room. Duffy wiped his brow. The mechs didn't have that kind of problem. They just stared at me with their eye cells. There was a dead silence.

"Now that I think of it," I said, "sticking around here and being General might not be such a bad idea after all."

CHAPTER 10

I got to the office early the next morning, bleary-eyed and groggy, a load of newspapers under my arm.

I put the office percolator to work brewing some coffee, plunked down in my swivel chair, spread the papers out on my desk and saw what there was to see. It wasn't a very heartening sight.

Headlines in four colors blazed at me. TOWN PLUNDERED! Another screamed: WAR! A third: CHAOS HITS HAPPY CITY! Nothing new there, except for the kind of chaos, which was just the messy sort Security Plus was supposed to prevent—and up to now, mostly had. "Can't win 'em all," a small, tired voice said in my noodle. An okay inscription for a tombstone, maybe, but not much comfort for anyone still left alive.

I sighed, got up, shuffled over to the percolator and poured myself a cup of coffee. What I really needed was a bottle of whiskey, but adding drunk and disorderly to my list of mounting troubles didn't seem like such a hot move.

I went back to studying the press, always a miserable job, even on good days. CONSTABLES ROUTED! another headline blared. Now that was more like it. A headline like that I could learn to live with, even grow to enjoy. So far,

Krimshaw's constables were taking most of the heat, at least
on page one; I didn't have the guts to dig deeper in the
papers. Not that it mattered much. The story was still young.
Once the air cleared, it wouldn't take the press and Tri-D
news hounds long to figure out who was really to blame for
all this. *Me*. Who else was there? Certainly not the bad
guys, nobody even knew who they were.

Miss Follsom, my chief junior exec, popped into the
office.

"Morning, boss."

She was a languorous, long-haired blonde, clad in a dia-
phanous, clinging, pale green dress. I put down my coffee
cup and gave her the attention she deserved, which, as usual,
was plenty. This, despite the fact that we spent a good many
nights together during the week, and most weekends, and
I had a pretty good idea what she looked like. For no reason
at all I started to feel better.

She waved a paper at me. "You see this, Thomas?"

"This" was a copy of the morning's *Daily Tattler* turned
to page six.

"Not yet," I said. "I've been saving that treat for last.
Something to look forward to."

I reached out, took her copy.

I'd made column two: SECURITY OP FELLS FEARSOME
FOURSOME. Without the picture underneath the headline
might've been taken as a compliment. The dumb picture
ruined it, of course. It showed me looking stern, as if I were
planning to run for D.A., and the four old coots I'd snared,
with their mitts raised high and broad toothless grins on
their lined pusses, as though they were tickled pink at the
thought of being collared. They looked as tough as minced
mackerel, but not half as dangerous. The story that followed
was a real doozy. My one hope was that *Tattler* readers
were too illiterate to get much beyond the photo.

"The good news," I said, "is that this didn't land on
page one. The bad news is what *did*."

"Forgive me for asking, Thomas—"

"Not if it's going to be something bad," I said.

"The morning news wasn't clear on this one little point."

"The morning news is rarely clear on anything. Along with the evening news. Only one point, eh? I bet it's a beaut."

She wagged her blonde head at me. "Where were you, sweetie, while our clients were taking this shellacking?"

"Out trying to make a living, kid, what else?"

"Any luck?"

I shook my head. "I didn't distinguish myself. But neither did anyone else on our side."

I told her about my scrap in Fearsburg. And what led up to it. Just telling it made me depressed all over again.

"My, you were busy," she said when I was done.

"Yeah. Idle hands lead to mischief; I wasn't taking any chances. Didn't do much good, though."

"It's plainly a conspiracy, Thomas."

"What isn't these days? You don't have to sell me on the notion, it's the board of directors, our clients, and everyone else in Happy City that'll need convincing."

She perched on the edge of my desk. "You have a plan, of course?"

"A plan? If you mean my retirement plan, I'm not eligible for another twenty-five years. I checked last night."

"Come on, Thomas, all these years in the business have given you scads of plans. Plans for *any* emergency, for all contingencies and occasions, right?"

"Yeah. Especially for birthday and wedding occasions, since I do catering on the side. But actually, I *do* have a plan for this mess." I leaned back in my swivel chair so I could get the full benefit of my colleague's inspiring view. "There's this opening for General in Fearsburg," I said. "Includes President-for-Life, Defender-of-the-People, Grand Vizier of Police, Chief of the Army, and Emperor, all rolled into one. You get to own half the stores in town, too, which is the *real* payoff. Beats heading up this crummy outfit, eh? So what I plan to do is sneak out the back door and apply for the job.

Guaranteed for life. That's usually not very long—they're on their ninth General now. But all jobs have their drawbacks. What this means is that as my chief junior exec, they'll probably name *you* president of Security Plus. So there's one question I must ask you, Laura: you got any good plans lately?''

She swung off my desk and into the client's armchair, crossed one nifty leg over another. "Let me put this simply. I have a plan, skipper."

"Skipper, yet. At least it's going to be simple; so few things are."

"Listen, Thomas, this whole Miklib business was engineered to sidetrack Security Plus, to get our mechs and ops far enough away from the scene of the crimes so they couldn't interfere; *you* were the bait."

I nodded thoughtfully. "You don't say? I'm old and tired, and probably verging on senility, but this *has* actually occurred to me, no kidding."

"Good for you, chief!"

"Yeah, chief. What I don't get," I said, "is why anyone should go to all this trouble."

"My question exactly. So before stopping in here, I asked the master computer."

"Old wire-brain?"

"Turns out, Thomas, the filched stuff adds up to more than it seems."

"I'm going to need a mathematician to figure this out, right?"

"Wrong, sweetie, I'll tell you."

"Damn straight of you, kid."

"Instruments of war."

"Eh?" I said brightly.

She repeated it.

"I'm sorry I asked."

"Bombs, cannons, aircraft, tanks," she said, "things like that. The parts can be made to produce them all. Especially if you've already got some other parts lying around."

I sighed. "I knew it was going to be complicated. War, yet. There hasn't been one of those since the Feds waved their white flag and went down the chutes."

"War, combat, battle, clashes, hostilities, *oodles of blood*, that's what the computer said. Or maybe the snatched items can be used for other things."

"Better. But not much. What other things?"

"It doesn't know."

I smiled grimly. "The master computer knows everything. It says so in its promo booklet."

"Not how to sew." She fixed me with her green eyes. "About war, though, it knows. So I would take the computer's analysis quite seriously, Thomas."

I shrugged a shoulder. "Maybe, but my money's still riding on those 'other things.' Listen, even certified psychos like the General've never tried to grab more territory. Their armies wouldn't stand for it. Look, lose a war and the army's kaput. All that fancy hardware down the drain. All the neat uniforms full of bullet holes. Lots of corpses lousing up the landscape. Top brass on trial as war criminals. All the perks gone forever; the mere thought brings a tear to my eye. I wonder why that dumb contraption picked war of all things?"

"A case of the smarts," Laura said.

"Yeah. We've all got the smarts, you, me, and it. No one's safe. So where are they gonna manufacture these stupid weapons? What plant's going to be converted? One in Happy City? Nothing illegal about making weapons, sweetie, there's just no great market for them these days. What's illegal is stealing the equipment to make 'em. And with all the spying devices handy, it's tough to keep a secret. Especially if you're converting a plant from making yo-yos and tin soldiers to something more interesting."

"What if it's not private enterprise, but some crazed city-state?"

I put my feet up on the desk, my hands behind my head, and gave her a neat, all-knowing smile. "Lots of crazed city-states out there. Only not crazed enough to call attention to themselves that way. Might make the other city-states kind of edgy."

"*Then* you'd have war."

I disagreed. "More likely a joint police action. That's when the surrounding city-states go in and level the offenders, along with everything else in sight. My guess is that won't happen, because this is a homegrown job. Fearsburg was just part of the scheme to get our mechs sidetracked, as you so shrewdly pointed out. No plants will be converted for war or anything else. That copped junk has another purpose."

"Which is?"

"Fancy detective work, my sweet, will ferret that out."

"So *that's* your plan!"

"Tried and tested, years of experience put to work on the problem."

"Thirty to be exact."

"More like sixty. I was referring to the dumb computer."

"And you?"

"Me? Think I'll go for a spin," I told her. "I've got it coming."

CHAPTER 11

Happy City looked like a patchwork quilt stitched together by the blind and palsied.

The downtown multi-shaped structures seemed embarrassed to rub shoulders together. The free-form buildings didn't belong next to each other, let alone the swanky glass-and-aluminum rectangles they shared space with. The brick and stone towers looked as if they came from some other, less advanced century—except for their size, which was too tall for *any* century.

Next to the Happy City skyline, I hardly had any troubles at all.

Tall buildings changed to three- and four-story town houses where the middling rich hung their hats and conspired to get even richer, a conspiracy shared by the rest of the town.

In their estates out in the suburbs, the super-rich schemed to hang on to it all. Tough to blame crooks for plotting to get a slice of the action, too. *I* certainly didn't; where'd I be without 'em?

I switched to mid-drive as I neared the tenement section known as Last Ditch Hollow. High-drive was too crowded with cars trying to bypass the area, and low-drive was too risky. Folks in the Hollow liked to pelt passing cars with dead rats, cats, and stones; the more ambitious residents did their target practice with guns. Mid-drive was safer. But being sandwiched between high and low was a test of nerve I always flunked. The sky seemed to be blotted out and engine sounds became a scream. A real boon for headache pills.

I floored the pedal, drove on for another couple of miles, turned left down a ramp, and found myself on ground level in Last Ditch. Who said I lacked character?

This was the west side, skid row's ritzy residential section. Farther east were the workingman's red light and gambling districts that specialized in bilking the poor. North and south was a kind of no-man's-land called the Dump, made up of ruined buildings, down-and-outers, muggers, and hopheads. Some of these dudes had lived in the west, visited the east once too often, and now ended up in the Dump.

The buildings here were only on their way to being ruins. They were weathered wood-and-shingle jobs set close together like a group of inmates from the Happy City Golden Years Club, too feeble to stand alone. They tilted at odd angles as though trying to avoid contact with each other. Garbage peeked out of trash cans as if hoping to be carted away from the neighborhood as soon as possible. It and me both.

I climbed out of my heap, stood gazing around.

A couple of guys shuffled by me eyeing the car as if it were some strange animal escaped from the zoo. There were some jalopies on the street; compared to mine they looked like candidates for the city dump. I'd need more than my magno locks to keep the vultures away. The only thing going for me was the early hour. Last Ditch didn't really get moving till mid-afternoon. I waylaid a couple of kids who should've been in school, and gave 'em ten bucks apiece to guard my vehicle. There was no one around I could get to guard the kids, so I went hunting for Jimmy Jimmy.

The bar on the corner was still closed, even here, but a greasy spoon was in business across the street. Faded lettering on the plate-glass window said GRUB. I moseyed over, pushed open the door. The place smelled of coffee, bacon and eggs rather than the swill I'd been expecting. The square wooden tables were empty except for a middle-aged woman in a flowered hat. Three customers, all men, were seated at the counter, chowing up. I slid onto a stool, joined them.

"Coffee, toast, and marmalade," I told the waitress behind the counter, a fortyish bleached blonde with penciled eyebrows and a dainty plastic apron.

She eyed me curiously, as if I'd asked when the next bank was going to be knocked over, but got my order anyway.

I took a bite of toast, a sip of coffee, and turned to the guy on my left. He was a tall, hefty joe with a seamed face and checkered lumber jacket. "I'm looking for Jimmy Jimmy," I told him.

He stopped eating his scrambled eggs long enough to stare at me. "Who?"

"Jimmy Jimmy," I said.

"What kinda name's that?"

"That's a very *queer* name," the waitress said.

"It's the three-dollar bill of names," I agreed.

A short, balding man on my right slapped his knee. "It's so queer, I can hardly stand it."

"What's he look like?" the tall guy asked.

I described him: a skinny, narrow-shouldered guy with slicked-back black hair, a long nose, pasty complexion, and squinty gaze, somewhere in his mid-thirties. Probably there were hundreds of guys around who fitted that description, but not all of 'em jammed into these couple of blocks.

"He means Jimmy the Fink," the short man said.

"That who you mean, mister?" the tall guy asked.

"Sounds about right," I told him.

"Jimmy the Stoolie?" The waitress made a face.

"Does kind of ring a bell," I said.

An unshaven elderly party by the wall said, "That Jimmy the Rat we discussin'?"

"Tag seems to fit," I said, "now that you mention it."

"You been keepin' *bad* company," Shorty said.

"Don't have his address, I suppose?" the tall man asked.

"Uh uh."

"Just know it's around here somewhere," he said.

"Yeah, that's about the size of it."

"That's Jimmy, all right," the short guy said. "Don't give his address to no one hardly. Gotta leave a message at the bar, right?"

"That's how it's done," I admitted.

"Wouldn't trust his own mother," the middle-aged woman in the flowered hat said from her table.

"That low-down rat'd fink on his own family for an extra buck," the short man said.

"Ain't got no conscience," the unshaven one said, rattling his coffee cup at me. "No sense of right, of decency."

"You seem like a *nice* sort," the woman said. "Why do you want to sully your hands by having anything to do with that shameless vermin?"

"It's business," I said, finishing my toast and coffee.

"Business?" the waitress said.

"What kinda business could you have with a skunk like that?" the short man asked.

"Want him to snitch for you, huh?" the unshaven one said. "To squeal, and tattle. *That* what you want?"

"Uh uh," I said. "He's already done that. What I want is to find out why he gave me a bum steer."

The woman said, "Is that what the big-mouth gave you? You paid him fair and square and he gave you a bum steer?"

"Whadda piece of work is man!" the waitress said.

"That fink ain't got no sense of right," the unshaven one said.

"Lucky you came to us, mister," the tall guy said. "You go to the grocery up the block, they take you for all you're worth."

"Now, here at Grub, we're reasonable," the waitress said.

"Like if you want a stoolie, and what man don't every now and then," the short guy said, "that's a ten spot."

"Apiece," the waitress said.

"Right," the tall one said. "And if you already got a stoolie and can't find him, that's twenty."

"Apiece," the waitress said.

"Well," I said, "there're five of you. That's a hundred smacks."

"The five who've got the dope," the unshaven one said. "Worth every penny."

"What happens," I asked, "when this place fills up? Everyone here gets a cut? You charge three grand or something?"

"Only us five in this racket, mister," the tall guy said. "Spend our mornings here. Bar opens at noon, that's when we goes outta business."

"Everyone asks the barkeep," the short guy said. "First place they head for."

"Would've done that myself," I said.

"Damn barkeep's even more expensive than we are," the waitress said.

Money changed hands; they gave me Jimmy's address.

"That's two-fifty for the chow," the waitress said.

I left the dough and a quarter tip.

"Big tipper," the waitress said bitterly.

I got out of there before I thought of another question to ask them and they really bankrupted me.

Jimmy Jimmy's dump was two blocks over. I hoofed it.
The sky matched the environment perfectly: a dirty
gray. The neighborhood was still mostly snoozing, so I
didn't have to worry about someone picking my pocket.
That left me with all my other worries, which were even
worse.

Odds had it that Jimmy Jimmy had set me up. And not
for kicks either. The four oldsters I'd collared were part of
the chain that led straight to Fearsburg, the looting of Happy
City, and worst of all, the P.R. mess I was in now.

Jimmy Jimmy was the key. All I had to do was make
him squeal. Pigs did it every day, but Jimmy might need
some convincing. I'd neglected to bring my thumbscrews,
and the old torture rack was too heavy to lug around. I'd
have to use more subtle ways to get at the truth. I hoped
I'd brought along enough cash. Though with Jimmy Jimmy
any amount was usually enough.

I stood across the street eyeing the house. Like all the
rest on the block, it'd seen better days. With all the dough
my outfit dished out to the guy, you'd think he'd've found
a better place to hang out by now. If for no other reason
than to make a visit like this more pleasant. On the other

hand, could anything make doing this more pleasant?

Gazing up at the crumbling, lopsided building, I began to regret not having sent a mech on this errand, a regret I was used to by now. Having mechs'd spoiled me. They didn't mind cooties, fleas, or bugs. If only I'd gone into another racket I might've been hobnobbing with the head of Happy City Industries right now. Probably as his chauffeur.

I took a step off the curb. And froze as solid as the Happy City Skating Rink in midwinter.

A black limousine had careened around the northwest corner, screeched to a jarring halt in front of Jimmy's house.

Four guys piled out of the car, ran into the building. They were big guys, dressed in flashy getups like boobs or thugs.

I stood stock-still, trying to imitate a lamppost. Any second I expected 'em to figure out their mistake, do an about-face and come running out to gun me down. Jimmy couldn't be the target. Not a moment before I was about to put the squeeze on him. Things didn't work that way. Some homing device must've been planted on me to guide 'em here. What better place than an empty street in Last Ditch to knock off the head of Security Plus? Only the guys had goofed, gone off in the wrong direction.

It made sense. Except for one small detail: so far the guys hadn't bothered to come back. I'd been bypassed again, wasn't the main attraction here. These birds were after different game.

Unless they really lived here. And had invested all their dough in a limo to impress their neighbors.

Fat chance.

I came out of my stupor, kicked into high gear. I dug my laser out of a pocket as I trotted across the street. Pushing open the front door, I plunged into semidarkness.

A winding staircase spiraled above me.

Four guys were barely visible between the third and top floor. They moved in silence, slowly, as if afraid that a misstep might topple the whole building. So far they'd done nothing bad. If they weren't after Jimmy Jimmy, this was none of my business. I wondered if I'd be able to explain that and back off before they blew a fuse.

I crept after 'em.

The four left the staircase, vanished somewhere on the fourth floor. By then I was on the second-floor landing, bent double as though hunting for bread crumbs. No one was shooting at me so I straightened up and began taking the stairs two at a time. I moved on tiptoes as though practicing a really tricky ballet step. I needn't've bothered.

I'd gotten past the third floor and was nearing the fourth when the boys pulled a fast one, proving yet again how tough it is to rely on anyone. Instead of going about their business in someone's flat and letting me peek through the keyhole, they were suddenly beating it.

All four appeared at the head of the stairs.

Too soon, I figured, for them to've gotten into trouble. Their hands were empty, while mine held a laser. I started to open my mouth to say something smart.

I never got the chance.

The four came right at me as if I were some wispy spook they could dash right through. They moved fast, pushing and shoving each other as if some large slobbering animal were nipping at their heels. I'd've been glad to step aside, but between them and the railing there *was* no aside.

"Hey, guys—" I began, raising my palm like some dumb traffic cop.

They plowed right into me.

The first two who'd been abreast of each other went down in a heap, along with me. The pair bringing up the rear had momentum on their side. They sailed over us as if hoping to sprout wings, and tumbled down the stairs to the third-floor landing.

The human knot I was part of began to wiggle. I was all set to do my bit and help untie it when an elbow jabbed me in the ribs. A fist freed itself from the tangle and cuffed me in the bean. I didn't like that. I slammed my laser against a forehead, put a knee in someone's stomach.

All I wanted was to quiet this pair, subdue 'em long enough to get away. Instantly things became worse.

Arms, legs, feet, and hands kicked, pounded and tore like some crazed centipede at war with itself. Teeth bit, mouths screeched. An annoying hand kept thumping my head against the wall. I burned it with my laser, was rewarded by a scream.

These crackers had gone ape. What I needed was a bunch of orderlies to strap them into straitjackets. What I had was my laser. I used it, swung again, connected with a nose, drove my foot into a chest, turned sideways and twisted free.

Falling back against the banister, I glanced up.

Jimmy Jimmy, in robe and pajamas, stood at the head of the stairs, his mouth half-open, his eyes staring, as though watching a cage full of unruly monkeys at the local zoo having a free-for-all. If he wondered what the hell was going on, he wasn't the only one.

My two playmates, meanwhile, had begun crawling down the stairs. I didn't see their pals. I stretched out a hand, grabbed one of the crawlers by the ankle. These joes didn't seem half as innocent now. A bit of chitchat was definitely in order. The guy screamed at me, kicked out.

As if on cue, a thundering noise shook floors, walls, ceiling, my teeth, and all the small change in my pocket.

The roof rose as if the house were tipping its hat to us.

Jimmy Jimmy flew by on the wrong side of the railing as if practicing a dive for the Happy City Aquatic Show.

A giant fist pounded my noodle into the floorboards.

Consciousness and I went our separate ways.

When I pried open my eyelids, things were quiet. I wasn't sure how much time had gone by. Not much, I figured. Even here, in Last Ditch, they had constables, firemen, and medics who responded to disasters. And what'd just happened had to be a disaster. I heard no sirens in the distance. Maybe only a minute had passed.

My two wrestling chums, I saw, were gone. A piece of sky looked down on me through a hole in the roof. I heard doors opening below, hushed voices.

Using what was left of the railing, I hoisted myself to my feet, stood there swaying. Nothing seemed to be broken, except maybe my spirit. The foursome hadn't come to lean on Jimmy, or shoot him dead, they'd come to leave a bomb on the landing and blow him up. But knowing that, I still didn't know anything—least of all how they'd gotten here a mere moment before me, and what I might've done to prevent it.

I shook off the plaster dust and debris and slowly started down. I wasn't exactly in tip-top shape. I'd've asked the tenants for a wheelchair or crutches, but they didn't look all that obliging. Doors closed as I staggered by. Eyeballs peered through cracks and peepholes. The staircase was all mine. In most parts of the city, tenants would be filling the hallways by now, looking for the injured, checking damage. Last Ditch was a bit different. No one wanted to be a witness here, even me.

I found Jimmy Jimmy down below. He lay crumpled like some abandoned, broken mannequin on the ground floor. I bent over him, hunting for some signs of life. "Jimmy," I said.

His eyes came open. "Dunjer."

"Take it easy, kid, help's on the way." It was, too; I could hear a siren in the distance.

He closed his eyes, sighed.

"Jimmy," I said, "who set me up?"

One helluva question to ask as a possible send-off. But a message for the Great Beyond would've probably depressed both of us even more.

He opened his mouth, licked his lips. "Mayor Strapper—" he began, his voice a faint whisper.

"Come on, kid, what about him?"

"His—"

"Yeah? Yeah? His *what?*"

Jimmy's mouth opened but no words came out. His head lolled sideways. No more wisdom from that direction—the kid had run out of answers, permanently.

I stood up. Like most of Jimmy's tips, his last one left a little something to be desired. Only this time it hadn't been his fault.

I went outdoors. The limo was gone. The sirens were growing louder. I had better things to do than explain to the constables and media what'd happened here. Especially since I had no idea myself.

I staggered around the corner and headed back to my car.

CHAPTER 13

"Dunjer," Mayor Strapper said, "you look like a house fell on you."

"You wouldn't believe me if I told you."

"Especially if you told me," he said. "It would have to be verified first by impartial observers."

"There aren't any in Happy City," I pointed out.

"Precisely. Now why are you bothering me in the middle of my workday? Don't you know I take a nap at this time every afternoon?"

"Trouble," I said. "That's why I'm bothering you."

"Trouble? You've come in the middle of my nap to discuss trouble? What are you, crazy? I have responsibilities, Dunjer, grave concerns that are listed here on this little official index card, this little card that I'm going to look at very soon, perhaps even tomorrow. You think it's easy running Happy City, trying to keep awake all the time? The last thing I need is trouble."

"You may not need it, Strapper, but you've got it."

"Not me. For trouble, you go to the vice mayor. Don't you know anything?"

Mayor Strapper's gilt-edged office was up on the four hundredth floor of the Happy City City Hall. This high up there ought to've been angels buzzing around, but only a stray bird and occasional copter poked its head through the clouds. At least the oxygen pipes were functioning today and I didn't have to wear one of the emergency masks. That made it almost a fun visit.

The mayor was medium-sized. He had a full head of white hair, gray eyes behind round glasses, and a gray mustache. A nice round paunch vaguely gave the impression that Strapper snacked on basketballs, which he swallowed whole.

He leaned back in his chair, eyed me morosely. "Go on, Dunjer, let's get this over with. Every few years some fool gets in here and tells me about trouble. Spoils my appetite for hours."

I crossed my legs, made myself comfortable in the visitor's chair. "Ever hear of a guy called Jimmy Jimmy?"

"Parents must have had a warped sense of humor. No."

"Guy was a stoolie."

"Was?"

"Just gone to his just reward."

"Alas," Strapper said. "The voters come, the voters go. Such is life, Dunjer."

"I'd always hoped there was a bit more to it," I said.

"Hadn't we all?"

"Uh huh. This Jimmy was bumped off."

"That's constable's work, Dunjer, not mine. Anything else?"

"Yeah, one small thing."

"Out with it, Dunjer, get it off your chest, you'll feel better."

"Sure, but will you? Before he died, Jimmy fingered someone."

"And you wish to share this secret with me? I'm touched, Dunjer, that you have such confidence in your mayor, but it's still constable's work; beat it."

"The guy he fingered was you, Strapper."

"Me?"

I nodded. "Said you'd set me up, got me out of town so all these plant lootings could take place. And the guy who did *that* probably had Jimmy killed, too."

He shook his head. "My dear Dunjer, there are many who bandy about the mayor's name in this town. For the mayor is tops in Happy City."

"Four hundred stories tops."

Strapper smiled. "As tops as one can get without a copter, or a Happy City jet. People claim they are friends with the mayor, work for the mayor, *are* the mayor. These people, Dunjer, are usually crazy. And for you to come here and bother me with this nonsense means that you must be crazy too."

I shrugged. "So you're innocent. Big deal. Your name was just the first word Jimmy uttered."

The mayor raised an eyebrow. "And what came after that?"

" 'His.' "

"His. That's all?"

"Uh huh."

"Very enlightening. His *what?*"

"My question exactly."

"*And?* Surely there is an answer?"

"Not from Jimmy. He didn't say."

"Didn't?"

"Couldn't. He'd died by then. But if not you, how about someone on your staff?"

"My staff? *That's* what you believe?"

I nodded. "They've got the know-how to pull off something like this."

Strapper waved his arm. "Go ahead, help yourself. Ask them anything you want. You're lucky, Dunjer, there are only four hundred floors of them. Start on any floor you like."

"Actually, I'd had something a bit less ambitious in mind."

Strapper gave me a long, level stare. "Such as?"

"Your vice and assistant mayors, your bureau directors, your immediate staff, something along those lines."

"Dunjer, why must it be *my* staff? Why don't you go pester some mayor in another city-state? Surely there must be one who would relish the attention."

"No doubt. But the plant knock-overs happened in this burg."

"We can arrange to have them happen elsewhere, can't we, Dunjer? Anything to have you go away."

"My going away won't get rid of the problem, Strapper," I said. "Look, I don't really think you're the culprit."

"I am gratified to hear it."

"You'd never let some harebrained scheme stand in the way of serious full-time snoozing."

"I'm glad we understand each other, Dunjer."

"But that doesn't go for your crew. Those guys are wide awake. They really run this town, are in an ideal position to get things done. And one of the things they might've got done is the swiping of those items."

"Why, Dunjer?"

"That's the question, all right, Mr. Mayor."

"And which ones did it?"

"That's the other question."

"You don't know," he said accusingly.

"Right. But we're going to find out."

"We?"

"You and me, pal. Listen, Strapper, all this happened on your watch. A scandal hits City Hall, you'll go down with the bad guys. Play ball with me, you'll come out looking like a hero."

"This ball I must play," the mayor asked, "is it strenuous?"

"Far from it. In fact, you do nothing."

Strapper beamed at me. "Now that's something I know how to do."

"Sure you do. All I need is your official say-so to go snooping around City Hall, interview some personnel, go through some files and records, maybe do a couple background checks. Stuff like that. You can sleep right through it.''

''*You're* going to do all that?''

''Uh huh. My boys from Security Plus.''

''Boys? What boys?''

''Mechs, actually. And a girl. A girl we've got.''

Strapper looked skeptical. ''The girl's all right, I suppose. But mechs are something else.''

''Sure they are. Only the best ops in the business.''

Strapper narrowed an eye. ''Better than *you*, Dunjer?''

''Let's not be ridiculous. Look, Mr. Mayor, trust me. Everything's going to be *all-l-l right*, you just wait and see.''

CHAPTER 14

"Well, Dunjer," Chief Constable Krimshaw rumbled at me, "I don't mind telling you I'm peeved."

I could tell he was peeved by the curl of his lips, the set of his jaw, the glint in his steel-gray eyes, and most important, the fact that he'd forgotten to square his shoulders and pull in his paunch for the hidden cameras in his office, a sure sign if ever there was one. Gone was the good-times getup, the toga and sandals. The chief constable was all business now, decked out in a no-nonsense dark blue uniform, with the simple words REELECT KRIMSHAW—LET'S NOT MESS AROUND emblazoned across his chest. A number of medals hung below the commercial. One looked suspiciously like it came out of a package of Yummy Snacks Breakfast Cereal, but what did I know?

"Taking a bit of flak, eh, Constable?" I said.

"A bit? They're hollering for my scalp!" He reached out a shaky hand to touch his bald pate, as if to make sure it was still properly attached.

I said, "Is there no justice, Krimshaw?"

The big galoot nodded. "Well put, Dunjer. They expect me to handle this whole mess! It's not the Happy City way to have government do it all!"

"How about some?"

"That's a matter of taste," the chief constable said, shrugging. "We constables are the symbol of law and order, Dunjer, and that's important. How'd I draw my paycheck without it? But everyone knows it's private outfits like yours that really carry the ball."

"Tell it to the Tri-D boys next time they ask you; we can use the plug."

"You think I'm crazy? What is it you want here anyway, Dunjer?"

"To speak with one of the old-timers I landed yesterday."

"Which one?"

"The one that makes the most sense."

"You're out of luck, none of them makes sense."

"Then choose one at random."

The chief constable reached for his phone, and chose.

"By cracky," the oldster said, giving me a broad, toothless grin, "ain't you the young whippersnapper that nabbed us?"

I admitted it.

"Well, let me shake your hand, pardner, you done us a real service, yes sir ree-bub."

We shook solemnly over the glass partition. They hadn't even posted a guard in the visitors' room. I could've slipped the prisoner a miniature laser easily, but why bother? The old coot *liked* it here.

"They treating you well?" I asked.

"By gum, it's a blast, sonny. Shoulda landed in the can last month. Gosh-darn wind near blowed me away."

"You're really happy to stay here, eh?"

"By jiminy, wouldn't think a stayin' no place else. That's loyalty, sonny. Place treats you good, you treat *it* good; only fair. You wanna be fair, sonny; makes folks think kindly of you."

"I'm sure the jail appreciates your business, Pop."

"Why shouldn't it? I'm an *old* friend. Old friends is best."

"And you regularly get pinched?"

"Regular as I can. Specially in winter."

"You weren't after cash in Cashville then?"

"Tarnation, sonny, what would I do with cash in here?"

"So you knew you were going to get caught?"

" 'Course I knew."

I looked at the old duffer. "How?"

"This here fella told me. He figured it all out for us. Now that was a *nice* fella."

"He got a name?"

" 'Course he got a name. What sorta darn-fool question's *that*?"

"Just checking. You wouldn't want to *tell* me his name, I suppose?"

"Now, sonny, I'd like to oblige. You done right good by us, ain't no two ways about it. But this here fella, he set the whole thing up, you know."

"Yeah, I know. And me too while he was at it."

The old fossil nodded. "Them's the breaks, sonny. Wouldn't be sportin' to snitch on him. What kinda world would this be, if folks snitched on each other?"

"The kind we've got right now," I told him. "Look, old-timer, maybe you don't know this, but the guy you're shielding is knee-deep in serious trouble."

"Didn't look like the ambitious type to me," the old codger said. "You sure?"

"Sure I'm sure. Don't let his looks fool you, Pop, he's slated for the big house."

"By snappy, the big house, is it?"

"Yeah, and as accomplices, you and your pals could keep him company."

He shrugged. "Worse places a body can be."

"Sure," I agreed. "Like out in the street." And leered at him knowingly.

"The street?" The old buzzard blanched. "Now you

wouldn't do a mean thing like that, would you, sonny?"

"Try me. I got you in, I can get you out."

The old geezer stared at me as if I'd sprouted horns and a tail and was about to jab him with my pitchfork.

"Well?" I demanded. "What's it going to be—a life of princely ease, or the rotten streets?"

He made up his mind quickly. "You drive a hard bargain, sonny. The fella's name was Mr. Jimmy."

"First or last?"

"Both."

I sighed. "He mention a guy called Spelville?"

"*Who?*"

"How about someone at City Hall?"

"You're barkin' up the wrong tree, Junior. He just gave us the layout and said we'd be caught. That was good enough for us."

Krimshaw's voice sounded through the hidden listening tube. "Want some help, Dunjer? I got ways to make them sing."

"Forget it, pal, it'd be off-pitch anyway. This guy thinks you're his benefactor, why disillusion him in his old age? Besides, he's telling the truth."

"No one tells the truth in here."

"Speak for yourself, Krimshaw."

"This is what we do," I said.

"We?" Laura said. "*Us?* You and I? Together? Facing danger, braving peril, taking on the bad guys in hand-to-hand combat, just like in the Tri-D suspensers? Is *that* what you mean?"

I nodded. "Very loosely. So loosely, in fact, the entire statement becomes meaningless."

"So," Laura said, "let's get down to brass tacks. Am I your sidekick or are you mine?"

I thought it over. "Actually, you're my frontkick. When it comes to combat, I like to have someone in front to take the first blast. Only reasonable, eh?"

"You're a laugh a minute, aren't you, you crazy kid you."

"Yeah, when I'm not sobbing hysterically."

"So what's this job you've got for me already?"

"I want you to scoot over to City Hall with a bunch of mechs. I'm betting that one of Strapper's helpmates is mixed up in our current crime wave. Start with the insiders and work your way down."

"How far down, kiddo?"

"Don't sweat it, Laura, not four hundred stories down. That far down you'd retire before the job was done."

"You had me worried, skipper."

My girl Friday had seated herself in the visitor's chair. She was decked out in a nifty pale blue print dress with orange, red, and yellow flowers on it, and a wide lacy collar.

"Yeah, skipper," I said. "The truth is you're really there for show."

"How nice. I'll wear my new dress."

"Not that kind of show, sweetie. For me tonight, you'll wear your new dress. For them, the object is to scare them."

"I'll go without makeup."

"That'll do it." I leaned back in my chair, made a steeple of my fingers. "Jimmy Jimmy fingered Strapper, but he never got to finish that all-important sentence. My hunch is, what would've come next was the name of one of Strapper's top joes. His boys run all those departments, can move truckloads of stuff around the city without anyone thinking twice about it. Private guys would need licenses, registration seals, tax stamps to set up shop somewhere. Strapper's guys are the ones who dish them out—to themselves as easily as anyone else. They're always emptying out and filling up buildings with equipment, and nobody cares what they're up to, least of all the mayor. So which one of these birds stands to profit from all this activity?"

"I should know?"

"You ain't the only one, honey. We'll have to do it the high-tech way—send some mechs over with you, have 'em hook up direct lines between our master computer and their computers at City Hall. It'll take some doing because they're really not centralized over there, but the blood, sweat and tears'll be worth it in the end; especially since mechs'll be doing it all and not us.

"We'll find out who Strapper's guys are, where they come from, what projects they're working on, stuff like that. And with that kind of dope, our computer here can do a complete background check on each of 'em, maybe dig out who they pal with, and who the pals buddy with. See if there're any skeletons in their closets. And, of real interest, of course, what their bank accounts look like."

Laura smiled sweetly. "And what will *I* be doing through all this, boss?"

"Running the mechs and interviewing Strapper's boys."

"The mechs hardly need running."

"Yeah, but it'll look good. The second part is the business end of the deal. We want to check any discrepancies between what the bureaucrats tell you and what our computer turns up. Meanwhile, our mechs'll be installing spotter eyes, catcher ears, and any other dirty little device that can help trip up the guilty at City Hall."

"But boss, almost *everyone's* guilty at City Hall."

"Keep it under your hat, kid. They figure out we're on to 'em, the whole government's liable to go on the lam."

CHAPTER **15**

I'd only been back from lunch for about five minutes when Krimshaw burst into my office, a bunch of constables at his heels. He still wore his fancy blue uniform but had added a visored cap that said CHIEF in bold letters. The cap spoke truth.

"All right, Dunjer, where is he?"

Krimshaw had finally done it. After all these years, he'd come up with a question that had me stumped; speechless, too.

"Eh?" I said.

"Spread out, boys," he boomed, "search the place."

The constables went right at it, just as if their chief hadn't taken leave of his senses. Most scooted back out the door to scour the whole suite. One peered under my desk, another opened my closet door, gave my overcoat, umbrella, hat, and galoshes the once-over. They probably didn't mind the company, but I was getting annoyed.

"Mind telling me what this is all about?" I said.

Krimshaw glared at me, sank into the visitor's chair. "You trying to tell me you don't know?"

I nodded. "That's what I'm trying to tell you. I was afraid you might not be able to figure it out."

"Part of Mech Industries has been hit."

I didn't have to dwell on that long—it was serious, all right. Mech Industries was where mechs constructed themselves. Dependable, trustworthy mechs—so far. In the wrong hands, though, renegade mechs could result, a result no one in their right mind would welcome.

"And you think I've got it stashed in my closet?"

"You don't understand, Dunjer."

"So enlighten me."

"The two top floors have simply vanished."

"You mean like carted off in trucks?"

"More like swallowed whole." Krimshaw dug a blue and red polka dote hanky out of his pocket, mopped his brow. "Gone, Dunjer—as if they never existed."

I gave him the old skeptical eye, the one I usually reserved for mech reports. "Surely you exaggerate?"

He laughed bitterly. "Go look for yourself. There were twenty-one floors this morning, now there are nineteen. We can only keep this hushed up for so long."

"Until someone learns to count, probably."

"Dunjer, this is the last straw. The public will never stand for it, they'll want blood."

"With renegade mechs on the loose, they won't have long to wait," I pointed out.

Krimshaw banged a fist into his palm. "It's *my* blood I'm talking about! Things have gotten out of hand. This'll be impossible to cover up, Dunjer; how will I ever explain it?"

A good question. "What you obviously need," I said, "is a fall guy, someone to take the heat for you. Hell, I'd be glad to do it—no kidding—but who'd believe me? Everyone knows I've got all the mechs I'll ever need. And if I could make things vanish, you'd be the first thing to go, Krimshaw, not some dumb factory."

"Very funny."

"So how come you're not laughing?"

"Look, Dunjer, there's no need to be disagreeable, it's not you I'm after."

A constable stuck his head into the office. "Place's clean, sir."

Krimshaw pulled himself to his feet. "No, Dunjer, the man we want was spotted entering these premises. But he's powdered out again."

The chief constable strode toward the door.

"You going to leave me in suspense, Krimshaw? Who is this mastermind of crime?"

"Humperdink Sass!"

"Eh?" I said, falling back on my patented comeback. This time my mouth was hanging open, too, an added dimwit touch, and genuine enough. Only there was no one there anymore to see I was stupefied.

I sat at my desk for a while longer, mulling it over. Any way I sliced it, it still didn't hang right. Dr. Sass, my old buddy, was noted for his invention of the activator, which let you travel through the doors of the universe from one continuum to the next. But no activators were around now, and Sass would hardly construct one, knowing what he did about the tricky little gadget. So what was all this about?

I rose, strode down the corridor and went into the room that housed the master computer. Or more precisely *was* the master computer. Knobs, dials, handles, slits, and blinking lights made it look like some giant pinball machine.

"Everything shipshape in here?" I asked.

"Order prevails," the master computer intoned. "As always."

"That's good. Have any company recently?"

"The constables. But we did not exchange pleasantries. They were, I'm afraid, quite at sea in my presence."

"I can imagine. How about before that?"

"Ah, you mean the strange little person with the tufts of white hair."

"Yeah, that's who I mean."

"He crawled into my storage chamber a few minutes after you went to lunch."

"Did he crawl out?"

"I certainly should have noticed."

I leaned over, pulled at a knob that resembled a few dozen others, and opened the concealed door to the storage area. "You in there, you slippery little devil?"

"Are they gone, Dunjer?" a voice called back.

"They are nincompoops," Dr. Sass said.

He was seated in my visitor's chair, the one just vacated by his nemesis. Sass was a small sixtyish man with a round, cherubic face. His head was bald except for two clumps of white hair that grew behind each ear. He had wide gray eyes and a short white Vandyke beard. He was wearing a light blue toga and yellow sandals this day, as good an outfit as any for crawling into storage spaces.

"They really think you did it?"

"Of course. I am their first and only suspect, it appears. Professor Gretch, my former pupil, works for Mech Industries. He managed to call before the constables obtained a gag order."

"Wasn't working on the top floors, I take it?"

"Only mechs up there, Dunjer—mechs constructing other mechs, a veritable orgy of wires, insulation, and stainless-steel hardware. Gretch says the constables are convinced that I have assembled another activator and used it to abscond with both floors."

"Why would you want to?" I asked.

The little man shrugged. "No doubt to start my own private army. As if I had nothing better to do."

"They don't know about the activator's minor drawback?"

"They know—it was well publicized at the time—but do they believe? That is the question. After all, it happened on other worlds."

The doctor was right. Nothing much had happened here

in Happy City. The activator had been flung into the fabric of the universe before disaster could strike. But the alternate worlds didn't fare half as well. In fact some of 'em went right down the tubes.

"Well, Doc," I said, "you've nothing to worry about."

"I don't? That is certainly news to me."

"Glad I could deliver it, then. Listen, you didn't go on that jaunt through Interworld all by your lonesome, did you? I was there, for one, and so were a couple of others. I'll round 'em up, Doc, we'll all testify about the bad things that happen when you use that gizmo. And, of course, no one's gonna find the top two stories of Mech Industries in your basement, are they?" I managed a small chuckle. "I sure hope not, anyway, and if my hopes are justified—and why shouldn't they be?—it'll all blow over."

The little man fidgeted in his chair. "But it won't."

"Blow over?"

"Precisely. Don't you see? Someone, somewhere *is* building an army."

I gave him a grin. "C'mon, Sass, don't let your imagination run away with you. There's no way you could know that."

"My dear Dunjer, you forget who I am."

"A true crackpot?"

"The world's leading authority on activators—possibly the only one."

"Yeah," I said, "and that's what got you into this pickle. So let's not make things worse by—"

"Excuse me," a voice said.

I glanced around. It took me a moment to realize the dumb alarm board had broken into our conversation.

"You again," I said. "This better be good, chum, or we replace you with a bevy of dancing girls and let the field take care of itself."

"I have monitored a report," the alarm board said.

"I'm glad you're keeping busy, the stockholders will appreciate it. This can't wait, eh?"

"That is entirely up to you."

"What's it about?"

"City Hall. My source was the constable's hot line."

"We tap into *that?*"

"We are tapped into everything."

"No one's safe," I said to Sass.

"At least you know who to blame," he said.

"Yeah, me. Don't rub it in. So what's the latest scoop, someone make off with the payroll?"

"Someone," the alarm board said, "has made off with the mayor's office."

"His office?" I said stupidly.

"Gone," the alarm board said, "along with the top three stories of the building, and everyone who was in it."

CHAPTER 16

"This is utter madness, Dunjer."

"Just hold tight, Doc," I assured him. "Everything's going to be *all-l-l right*." The last guy I'd told that to had been the mayor and look what'd happened to *him*. I decided not to even think about it. Worse thoughts were crowding my mind.

I saw an opening up ahead and gunned the cycle between two speeding cars. The cycle knew how to move. Only a copter might've been faster, but coming in for a landing near a disaster site was a bit touchy; constables would be all over the place. With Sass aboard, I couldn't risk it. My leading expert on these catastrophes was also the most wanted man in town. I didn't intend to lose a celebrity like that to a jail cell. Not yet, anyway.

I had my passenger shrewdly disguised in Hogart's tan raincoat. Hogart was a short, paunchy human op whose coat was a reasonable fit. And except for the sandals, and the blue toga sticking out and fluttering underneath, the doc looked almost normal. Or as normal as the doc could look, which wasn't very. I'd added a brown muffler, dark glasses, and a gray fedora to his getup, somehow making the little guy even more conspicuous.

The way Sass was clinging to my back, I felt as if I'd grown an extra appendage.

"There is absolutely no need for my presence," he hollered into the wind.

"Sure there is," I hollered back. "You're the last straw I'm going to grasp at."

"Talk sense, Dunjer!"

I saw another opening ahead between a truck and car, and squeezed us through. The problem with cycles was staying alive long enough to enjoy the ride. I was doing my best, but the rest of the traffic would have to hold up its end. "Miss Follsom, our junior exec, was up at City Hall," I said, "along with a squad of mechs."

"Unfortunate. You will have to replace the whole lot, I fear."

"Can't do that, Doc, Miss Follsom is irreplaceable."

"Nonsense, Dunjer, no one is irreplaceable, with the possible exception of myself, of course. Some mech will simply have to take over her duties."

"They wouldn't know how, take my word for it."

"You may have no choice, Dunjer."

"Sure I do. We'll simply find out which Happy City bigwig is pulling this rotten stunt and go spring her."

"Dunjer, the activator cannot move objects from one place to another like some trucking firm."

"It can't?"

"Of course not. The activator only moves objects to different worlds."

I spied an opening on high-drive, made an illegal right turn, heard brakes squealing on all sides of us, and roared up the ramp. If I could survive that turn, I could survive anything—even Sass. "And this has gotta be the work of an activator, you say?"

"Certainly. What other explanation is there?"

"You're the expert, Doc, that's why you're along. But I thought that once you use that thingamajig, everything blows up, sinks, falls into a sun—"

"Or something equally unpleasant. Of course. But not always."

"Not?"

"Theoretically, it *is* possible, at least temporarily, to shield an activator."

"Since when?"

"All along, I suppose. Up until now the issue was quite academic. *I* certainly wasn't about to build another activator. But someone has, Dunjer, or somehow obtained one."

Off in the distance I caught my first glimpse of City Hall. The tower was surrounded by other towers, clouds, copters, and, at that height, probably angels on the wing. It didn't look especially dwarfed from here and I wondered if this whole thing could be an error. It wasn't likely. For it to be an error, not only the constable's hot line had to be wrong, but our communos—which got no answer from the Hall— all had to be on the blink. All was too many, even for Security Plus.

"I thought there were no activators left," I said.

"There aren't. They were abandoned somewhere in the fabric of the universe. That's the whole point. I am convinced that all our troubles stem from *out there*."

"Covers a lot of ground, Doc."

"More than you imagine. I do not mean the alternate worlds that form the continuum. They would be only a remote possibility, provided someone had constructed a shield."

"Remote? Why?" I asked.

"Because a shield on those worlds would only be temporary at best. Disaster would strike sooner or later. Sooner probably. Before a war could be carried to completion."

A clear stretch of roadway loomed ahead of us. I put on a burst of speed, covered a quarter mile in nothing flat, and zoomed down a long ramp toward Happy City's municipal center.

"What does that leave us with, Doc? It's not here, and it's not there. So where is it, in between?"

"You have hit on it, Dunjer."

"I have?"

"Indeed. I shudder to say so, but I am afraid there is only one logical place: *a specter world.*"

Happy City's school system must've been better than I remembered, it's graduates *could* count. There was a whole crowd of 'em gawking and gaping up at City Hall. The constables had roped off the area, put up barricades, as if the culprits were still hanging around, planning to smuggle the top floors out piece by piece.

I climbed off the cycle, turned to my passenger. "Well, what do you think?"

The little man removed his dark glasses, gazed up at the building. "You see, Dunjer—gone, as if they never were."

"Yeah, never were. So what's your learned prognosis, Doc? Your gizmo do this?"

"Hardly *my* gizmo, Dunjer; mine no longer exists. But if you mean is this the work of an activator, assuredly."

I nodded. "Okay, stick around, I'll be back in a jiffy. This crowd ought to give you enough cover. Just don't look too sinister."

"It wasn't my idea to wear this ridiculous costume."

I left Sass guarding the cycle and went hunting for the law. I recognized a number of constables. Krimshaw wasn't among them yet, which was fine with me. I spotted Detective Dawson whom I knew from way back, and went over to him. Dawson was a sturdy six-footer with a large walrus mustache and ruddy complexion. We swapped hellos.

"Anyone around from the mayor's office?" I asked.

"You're in luck," he told me.

I was led over to a teenage kid, standing with a bunch of cops. "Office boy," Dawson said. "Was sent out to run an errand."

I introduced myself to the kid. "Son," I said, "a bunch of mechs and a pretty lady show up this morning?"

"You mean Miss Follsom, the blonde bombshell?"

I nodded.

"Whatta tootsie!"

"She with Strapper when you left?"

"Interviewing the staff, man. She hadn't gotten to me yet. Now it's too late."

"How's that?"

"She was on the top floor. It's bye-bye birdy. And me but a few days away from full maturity," the kid said.

"Get what you wanted?" Dawson asked.

I sighed. "What I didn't want."

A nice crowd had collected around Sass when I got back. He had official company, too, Krimshaw and some of his cronies. The chief constable had a large hand on the little man's shoulder. "So, Dunjer," he said, "harboring a dangerous fugitive. I knew it all along."

"Grow up, Krimshaw, this guy's the solution, not the problem. Besides, he was with me the whole time City Hall was being nabbed."

"You admit it then?"

"Yeah, and I'll testify to it in court."

"You'll get your chance, Dunjer. I'd run you in too, but Security Plus has too many lawyers on its payroll."

"They'll all be on the Sass defense team," I warned.

Krimshaw shrugged. "It's a free city, Dunjer, do what you want. Just because our friend here was with you doesn't mean he couldn't have had accomplices."

"But to what purpose?" Sass asked.

"Rule our glorious little city-state, of course."

"How tedious," Sass said.

"Tell it to the judge!" Krimshaw roared.

CHAPTER 17

Carrot-topped Ed Morgan shook his head. "I'm a lawyer, not a jailbreaker."

"One of thirty under contract to Security Plus," I reminded him. "If you can't spring Sass, some of our other boys will."

"Want to bet?"

I mentally sorted through my finances. "Not at the moment," I said.

"You're smarter than you look, Dunjer."

"That's not saying much," I pointed out. "Sweet-talking me won't get you anywhere, Morgan. If we don't move on this, Security Plus is a goner."

I was back in my office, Morgan seated in my visitor's chair. The place seemed orderly enough. Mechs, alarm board, and master computer still went about their business of safeguarding our clients. But for all the muscle they had now, they might've been stuffed dolls.

"You're trying to tell me something, Dunjer. That a city without its City Hall, not to speak of its trusted mayor, is in trouble."

"I don't think anyone's ever trusted Strapper," I said.

"That the unknown forces arrayed against Happy City are growing in power."

I shrugged. "We can handle that—with the right know-how behind us."

"That I'll have to take a pay cut if I don't do this right."

"That's a thought," I said. "Actually, I was thinking of Miss Follsom. Morale around here—mostly mine—won't be worth beans till we get her back. And as the guy who runs this show, I gotta be kept happy. Otherwise, it's the skids."

Morgan leaned back in his chair. "If Sass is the key, forget it. Krimshaw won't budge on this."

"Krimshaw? Come on, pal, what about the D.A., the Chief Justice?"

Morgan gave me a small smile. "You forget their locations, Dunjer."

"Hmmmm, three hundred and thirty-eighth floor, eh?"

Morgan nodded. "Krimshaw's the surviving legal authority. And he's convinced Sass is behind all this. He won't budge."

"That's not so hot."

Morgan scratched his head. "I suppose I can always go back to my old job at Underwood and Snow," he said, "if things went to pieces here."

"Didn't they have you dusting their offices between cases?"

"Only on weekends."

I cast a long glance out my window. Off in the distance, what was left of City Hall was still standing tall. Too tall. Another three hundred and thirty-seven stories to go and the city would be minus one more eyesore. But would the culprits come back and do the job right? "Well," I told Morgan, "there might not be an Underwood and Snow left when all this is over. Or a Dunjer and Morgan, either."

"We're all changing our names?"

"If Sass is right," I said, "someone's planning an all-out war against Happy City."

"Wars are obsolete."

"Were, Sass says."

"And if he's wrong?"

I laced my fingers. "We keep muddling along as usual."

"War," Morgan said, "might actually be an improvement."

"Especially if it happens somewhere else. That's the problem. It won't."

"Maybe this will help."

"Nothing'll help."

Morgan leaned over, placed a small wrapped object on my desk.

"What's that, an aspirin?"

"Tape cube."

"Aspirin would've been better."

I unlaced my fingers, peeled paper off the cube, touched it gently with a forefinger. "This is Sass," the tape said. "Your Mr. Morgan has informed me that I may be in this loathsome place indefinitely."

"If not longer," I told the cube, which ignored me.

"It is therefore up to you, Dunjer," Sass said. "Total anarchy may strike the city at any moment. And on its heels, murderous invading armies. You must stop them."

"I was afraid he'd want something hard," I told Morgan, "like fresh orange juice with breakfast in his jail cell."

"No one could want anything *that* hard," Morgan said.

"True," I admitted.

"You must journey beyond Happy City," Sass said, "in search of our enemy."

"I got plenty of enemies right here," I told Morgan.

"Who hasn't?"

"Beyond even the worlds of the continuum," Sass said. "Perhaps to the dreaded specter worlds themselves."

"How far is that?" Morgan asked.

"Not within walking distance."

"Only one man, besides myself, can possibly assist you in this undertaking," Sass said. "He is Professor Nigel of

Tech City. Somehow, you must reach him; he must be persuaded to help. Not only the fate of Happy City hangs in the balance, Dunjer, but perhaps the fate of the entire world. Or even the universe. Who knows? One thing, however, is abundantly clear. *I* will doubtless remain in this wretched hole until evidence is brought back to clear me. And the best evidence is *out there*. So even if the universe is *not* at stake, you know where your duty lies. Good luck, Dunjer, and, of course, I shall be quite happy to remit your standard fee, minus the usual ten percent reduction for previous clients.''

I grinned sourly at Morgan. ''I figured he'd want me to do it for free.''

''That's the worst load of gobbledygook I've heard in years,'' Morgan said. ''War, the whole world at risk, maybe even the universe. Still, you *are* getting paid.''

''A big nine hundred bucks. Provided the job takes a whole week and the universe doesn't blow up in the interim. It blows, I don't get any fee at all.''

''You really signing on?''

I nodded. ''Can't do any less for the old universe, pal. Or Happy City. Or even you and me. But especially Laura Follsom. Her I bring back if it's the last thing I do.''

''Then you believe the little crackpot?''

''I've been out there, Morgan. I've seen what can happen on the alternate worlds.''

''You're even crazier than he is.''

I shrugged. ''It's gonna be tough. Without an activator, there's no way to breach the fabric of the universe. Sass had the only ones, they're gone now, and the damn things take years to build.''

Morgan thought it over. ''Maybe this Nigel will have the answer.''

I smiled mirthlessly. ''And you think *I'm* crazy.''

''The Happy City Jet?'' Captain MacKrack said.
''Gotta have it. It's a matter of life and death. But I

promise to bring it back in one piece. Scout's honor."

We stood outside his wooden shack, the airstrip behind us. The tarmac was cracked and pitted, but so was the jet. At the moment, the object under discussion wasn't on display for the high-school kids. It was resting in its battered hangar, probably with a hangover.

"I'd be only too glad to loan it to you, lad," the captain said. "You know that."

"I do?"

"But that's impossible."

"I was hoping for improbable."

"That's if the mayor were around. With him gone, it's impossible."

"MacKrack," I said, "the mayor would *want* you to loan it to me. How'm I gonna get him back if you don't loan me the jet?"

"It's not just that I'm bound by regulations, lad."

"It's not?"

"Motor sprang a leak."

"So fix it."

"We tried. Took the damn motor apart piece by piece. Then put it together again."

"And they say you're a maladroit."

"Don't work a lick now. How about I rent you a *nice* copter?"

"Won't do, MacKrack."

"Too mundane for you, lad?"

"Too easy to shoot down, Captain."

"Now who'd do a mean thing like that?"

"Just about anybody, these days."

"Theoretically," the master computer said, "it is possible."

"How about practically?"

"Such an expedition could have only one outcome. Security Plus would be in the market for a new president."

"That bad, eh?"

"Considering the fact that that very peculiar little person and I have both predicted the likelihood of imminent war—which would no doubt destroy *everything*—who is or is not president of this insignificant organization cannot truly be deemed a pressing matter. Therefore the word 'bad' is hardly relevant in this context."

"Righto, you creep."

"The master computer just nixed an armed expedition," I told O'Tool, "even through the more benign city-states."

"There are no benign city-states, just lesser evils," O'Tool said.

"We could always try to negotiate safe passage through the lesser evils," I said. "But even with the mayor here, heading up our negotiating team, it could take months."

"And years with him gone."

O'Tool was a hatchet-faced human op with hooked nose, hooded eyes, and thin lips. We rented him out to scare juvenile delinquents. Otherwise he did the usual human op turns: appeared on Tri-D to tout our mechs, dug up and paid off our string of stoolies, testified in court against felons, and tried to avoid shoot-outs with bad guys.

"So what do you think?" I asked him.

O'Tool held up a finger. "Only one thing to do."

"Get a new master computer?"

"The underground railroad."

"A metaphorical moniker for a clandestine cloak-and-dagger outfit?"

"Only in a manner of speaking."

"Yeah," the trucker said, "all youse gotta do's lie still, palsy. In there." He nodded toward the large oil rig.

"For how long?"

"Coupla hours."

"You got a license for this trip?"

"Inter—city-state. For th' oil, palsy, not youse."

"I climb into a tank full of oil?"

"Youse climbs inta th' tank under th' tank full a oil."

"Hidden, eh?"

"Whadya think?"

"What happens when we hit Niceville?"

"Simple, palsy. I pays off th' border guards, th' customs guards, th' highway guards, an' th' Niceville Oil Warehouse guards."

"I thought you had a license?"

"Sure. No license, they shoots youse."

"What happens then?"

"I drags youse outta th' tank, sees if youse still breathin'—ha, ha, just kiddin', palsy, no one's croaked on me yet; almost. Ticker okay?—dress youse up like in Niceville, that's wid one a them lace an' ruffles getups, see, steer youse across town, and inta th' ol' railroad tunnel. Gotta railroad car stashed there. I puts youse inna driver's seat, waves bye-bye, an' youse home free, palsy. 'Cept it ain't free, 'cause our guys gotta pay off all a them gov guys inna four states youse passin' under. Tunnel's supposta be closed, only it ain't. Lotsa guys gettin' rich off'n th' tunnel; they keeps tabs real good. That's how come th' trip's so expensive, palsy. Youse in Goodsville now. Got lotsa chain gangs in Goodsville, but that's better'n th' firin' squad, huh? We dresses youse up like a lil' ol' lady—no one's gonna put no lil' ol' lady on no chain gang, most days—an' gets youse to th' border. Truck's waitin' for youse there. Crawl under th' load a apples—border guards been paid off—an' it's Tech City here youse comes. Nothin' to it, palsy."

CHAPTER 18

"**Y**ou must come out," the metallic voice grated.

I was having a terrible nightmare. I dreamed I was suffocating under a ton of apples, and a grating metallic voice was giving me orders. What could be worse?

Slowly I opened my eyes. Darkness. And the unmistakable odor of apples. I had my answer: *this* could be worse.

"I know you are in there," a voice called.

Some dream. It came after you even when you were awake. A disagreeable object had begun poking me in the ribs. I grabbed hold of it with one hand, clung to my package with the other, and hoisted myself up through the load of apples till I hit daylight. Only it wasn't daylight.

I was still on the cargo truck, all right, but the vehicle wasn't outdoors anymore. I was in a gigantic metal-walled room. Huge spotlights shone down from the distant ceiling, reflected off the four walls. I shielded my eyes against the glare, took a quick look around. A rectangular slab of metal loomed over the truck, was wielding a pole in one of its eight appendages. A utility mech. Happy City used a few in factories, but basically preferred the humanoid type—as though it made a difference.

"Do you possess an entry permit?" the slab demanded,

in a voice that had all the charm of two tin cans clanging together.

"No, but—"

"You will be expelled," the slab told me. "To Goodsville, as that is the nearest point of entry."

"Listen, pal—"

"A male human in the prime of life," the slab continued, "has a life expectancy of eight point three years on the chain gang. You, of course, will have much less."

"Thanks loads. Look, I'm not gate-crashing, I'm here on official business."

"What is your name?"

"Dunjer."

An instant's pause. "I have scanned the visa lists, your name is not among them."

"Yeah, there was no time for formalities, this is a class-one emergency. I'm here to see Professor Nigel."

"In reference to what?"

"I bring a message from a colleague of his, Dr. Sass of Happy City. Top priority. Urgent. Red alert. Also, it can't wait another instant."

I hoped the magic name of Sass did the trick. I didn't think I'd like the chain gang.

The slab was silent for a moment. I reached for an apple absently, but put it back. After my trip, apples had lost a good deal of their appeal.

"Professor Nigel has agreed to speak with you," the slab announced.

"Good. Take me to him."

"Sit."

High above my head, part of the right wall receded into itself, revealing a large screen. A giant head peered down at me. "Yes, what is this about Sass?" a voice boomed.

"He's gotten himself pinched," I shouted. "And one of his activators is on the loose."

"No need to shout," the large head said. "Are you quite sane?"

"Yeah," I said, "last time I looked."

"Why are you dressed like that?"

"The lady's getup? I'm in disguise."

"Why?"

"To get through Goodsville in one piece. Don't you know that?"

"How should I? I have no desire to get through Goodsville. Better come see me at once."

"That was the idea."

The slab sent me by underground chute. I didn't go unescorted, either. Spotter eyes lined the tunnel, made the old Happy City surveillance network look the minor leagues. I got my own clothes out of my package, changed into them. A mech voice told me when to rise from my seat, step off the mobile strip. A speed lift carried me up.

The man who met me by the study door wore a dark green paisley dressing gown over a yellow striped shirt and tan trousers. He was medium height, wiry, and fiftyish. His forehead was lined, his salt-and-pepper mustache, bushy. Hair and eyebrows were jet-black, cheekbones high, eyes cool green, and aquiline nose long and tapered.

We exchanged hellos. I was ushered into the study and nodded toward an armchair. Nigel sat across from me, sunk in a black easy chair. Three walls were lined with books, tapes, and disks. A computer terminal sat on a corner table. The fourth wall was glass and looked out on the city. I saw tall, slender structures with domed appendages glittering in the sun. They were all made of polished metal. Narrow metal skyways spiraled around the tallest of the buildings, wound away and were lost somewhere in the city. A few copters bobbed in the clear air. Some ground cars scooted along the gleaming skyways. I couldn't spot a trace of grime or pollution.

"Keep it clean out there, eh?" I said.

"Immaculate. Self-polishing, you know."

"I didn't."

He nodded. "Tech City, after all. Self-polishing won't help a jot if Sass's activator has fallen into the wrong hands."

"Think maybe you can help?"

"Not if you don't tell me precisely what's happened, Mr. Dunjer."

"Just Dunjer will do."

"Get on with it, man."

I got. Nigel sat perfectly still, his hands calmly folded in his lap, peering at me intently as if I were a chess piece in an especially tough position. I gave him the facts—something I knew how to do pretty well. Years of writing reports and trying to bilk the last penny out of clients had turned my delivery into an art from.

I stuck in as many fine points as I could remember. I didn't have a clue what, if anything, might turn out to be useful. When I was finally done, I tossed him Sass's voice cube, evidence, of a sort, that I wasn't talking through my hat. Some evidence. While he listened to the cube, I sat back in the armchair, sighed, and stretched out my legs. I'd done it, gotten to the expert and given him the lowdown. Now it was his baby—he could get busy and save the universe. Or at least the small part of the universe that was Laura. I'd settle for that.

Nigel closed his eyes when the cube had said its piece, sank even deeper into his chair, and was silent.

When nothing happened for a while, I said, "Professor?"

"I'm thinking," Nigel said, his eyes opening. "It always impresses the students."

"Yeah, I'm impressed too. Especially if you come up with something that's not half bad."

"My dear Dunjer, not half bad is my dish of tea."

"That's a load off my mind."

"However, I should mention, it's all theoretical."

"Yeah," I said, "Sass uses that word too. Usually when he's stumped, and doesn't know what to do."

"Theoreticians are rarely stumped in that way, Dunjer, since they almost never *do* anything."

"Great."

"However, only one of us is a theoretician."

"You've got a job for me, eh?"

"One requiring a man of action, of consummate skill, of unquestioned courage."

"Someone willing to put his life on the line, I bet."

"I couldn't have put it any better."

"Sure. That's what they always want."

"Ah, but this time it's different, Dunjer."

"We hire someone to do it instead of me?"

"*All* our lives are on the line."

"And I got to save 'em all, eh?"

"Not alone, my dear Dunjer. I do dabble on the practical side, too."

I looked at the guy. "That mean you'll lend a hand?"

"I have a choice?"

"So what do we do?"

"Kidnap the Splat sisters."

I didn't get to see much of Tech City this time around either. We used the chutes again, a mobile strip hustling us along at a smart gallop. A small, squarish utility mech with four wheels and eight extendible appendages kept us company, lugged a couple of bags full of clothing. We were going on a trip, but I doubted it would be a fun-filled outing.

"How come you people don't humanize your mechs?" I asked.

"Less obtrusive this way," Nigel said. "And they don't prattle."

"Yeah. Well, before I take my vows of silence like our little pal here, maybe you can tell me something."

"Out with it, Dunjer."

"Tell me you know about activators, Professor. Just to make me feel better, eh?"

"Here in Tech City, to make you feel better, we give

you a pill, not answer silly questions. The whole world knows that one of my papers laid the theoretical basis for the activator. Or would know if we weren't divided into these asinine little city-states."

"You had me worried, Prof, I was afraid you wouldn't know how to build one fast."

"I don't. Or even slow. Theory and practice, my dear Dunjer, are two distinct realms. Even with the considerable technology of Tech City behind us, it would be hit-and-miss. For months if not years."

"So how we gonna nab the troublemakers?"

"With an activator, of course."

"There aren't any."

"Not in this time zone."

We surfaced at an airstrip. The city was off to the side and I could see grassy fields around us beyond the tarmac. Unlike the Happy City airport, there was no ramshackle shack to report to, only a modern steel-and-glass domed structure that glistened in the sun. Obviously, these people had no respect for the past. There were plenty of planes parked in the glass hangar. For all I knew, they could even fly.

"Nice fleet you've got here," I said.

"It discourages aggressors. This way," Nigel said, taking off at a trot.

He skirted the domed building, headed straight for the hangar. The utility mech and I scrambled after him. A mechanic in grease-stained overalls and two guys in uniform passed us going the other way. All three saluted.

"You in the military?" I asked.

"Something far better, a scientist. Tech City, after all."

"Uh huh. They know you by sight?"

"Of course. My work often takes me aloft; I have my own ship here."

"Copter?"

"Heavens no."

"Jet, eh?"

"Not quite."

"Magic broomstick?"

"Spaceball."

"Quit kidding, Prof."

I floated out of my chair, stretched out a hand and pulled myself back.

"Jeez," I said.

"Try not to hurt yourself, Dunjer, I'm going to need you."

"Yes sir."

We were in a white metal ball. Nigel had simply ordered the ship towed out onto the field, as one might order a chocolate sundae at a soda fountain. He went up a ladder, opened a hatch, and climbed aboard. I followed.

"Strap yourself in," he said.

I strapped. Nigel took the controls, radioed for and received clearance, and touched a knob. Jets shook the ball, blasted us up like a giant cork popping out of a champagne bottle. It took me a while before I was able to drag my stomach out of my toes. Catching my breath, I glanced out a porthole, became dizzy all over again. Below us the earth was slowly sinking away.

"Use the waist strap, Dunjer," Nigel said. "It will keep you anchored."

"How come I've never heard of this thing?" I asked. "You'd think word would get around."

"Classified. Tech City is a closed book, Dunjer. In a world such as ours that is the only sensible course. If the Governing Board knew that I was planning to land this ship near three city-states, they would be up in arms."

"Three?"

Nigel nodded. "The Splat sisters, you see, are triplets."

"Actually, I don't see."

"They are the only ones who can help us find an activator."

"They find things?"

"Only in a manner of speaking. They were separated as teenagers, once their specific ability became known. This was shortly before the Federal Government ceased to be. We in Tech City were instrumental in dealing with the problem."

"There was a problem, eh?"

"Oh, yes. Individually, the three sisters were distinguished only by their thorough dislike of one other. Together they were something else."

"Triple-threat femme fatales?"

"Psychic, my dear Dunjer. That is singular, not plural. They functioned only as a unit. Distance from each other rendered them harmless, which is what society wished them to be. Now, for the good of society, they must be reunited. Peaceful Haven is our first stop."

"Better Peaceful Haven than Strangleburg, eh?"

"Perhaps not. Unfortunately, not everyone in Peaceful Haven is peaceful."

CHAPTER 19

"I don't think I like it here," I said.

"Who does?" Nigel asked.

"No one?"

"Stupefied is the usual condition of these people. The trouble is, you're awake, Dunjer."

"Yeah, I knew there was trouble somewhere."

"Shhhh," he said.

A squad of armed, sharp-eyed cops had just turned a corner, began swaggering toward us in mid-street half a block away. Any place that had its cops patrolling in squads was a place to steer clear of. No traffic got in their way either—mainly because there wasn't any. Peaceful Haven had all the get-up-and-go of a corpse.

Three-story brick buildings lined both sides of the block. They looked old and tired, like the few citizens we'd passed. I did my best to look that way, too. A half hour in this burg made it seem easy.

The cops' eyes raked us over, picked us clean like vultures dining off a cadaver, saw we were docile enough, and moved on to other suspicious sights.

We moved, too.

Nigel and I wore the standard outdoors regalia for these

parts: long-flowing white gowns and sandals. We both carried black backpacks. Our steps were slow and languid, just
like the few other pedestrians we'd seen. We kept our eyes
half-lidded, sleepy. The spaceball was parked back in a
semi-wooded area a couple of miles from town, obviously
the preferable place to be.

A guy drifted out of one of the brick houses, began
heading our way.

Nigel halted, held up a hand, palm out, as the chubby,
middle-aged party approached us. "Peace, brother."

The guy ground to a stop, tried to focus on us. "Peace,"
he said uncertainly, as though he wasn't quite sure what the
word meant. He wasn't the only one.

"We are rustics." Nigel enunciated slowly as though he
had just learned the language. "We seek Bliss and Comfort
streets."

You could all but hear the gears painfully clicking away
in the guy's noodle. Something that could have been a light
appeared in his cloudy eyes. He began giving us halting
directions; it took a while, as if he were explaining some
intricate scientific principle he wasn't sure we could quite
grasp. Luckily, we were only a couple of blocks away, or
we'd have been stuck there all day.

The guy finally drifted off. We continued on our trek. I
said, "Water supply, eh?"

"Not just the water," Nigel said. "In Peaceful Haven
they don't do things by half measure."

"Mechs run the industries?"

He nodded. "The people certainly couldn't."

"So who profits?"

"The Swami."

"Dictator for life?"

"Eternity, to hear him tell it."

"Nothing like the long view."

The row of houses was on a side street, set apart. They
had all they could do to keep from toppling over, were made

of weathered, unpainted planks. Shingles had once covered the roofs. A few were left like stray teeth in an oldster's mouth, useless reminders of better times.

"Your pal lives in a slum?" I asked.

"Used to be an exclusive section," Nigel said. "Reserved for the star achievers."

We stopped before a house that looked like all the others. He knocked. After a while the door slowly came open as if resisting the force of gravity. The old man who stood before us in wrinkled white shirt and baggy white trousers was white-haired, stooped. He wore a long white beard. Faded hazel eyes peered at us out of a creased, bony face.

"Patrick?" Nigel said.

The man opened his mouth. "Uh?" he said.

"It's Nigel," the prof said, a hint of irritation in his voice.

The oldster nodded vacantly, as if he'd been told we'd come to read the gas meter. The door opened wider.

We went in, silently trooped down a long hallway, entered a musty sitting room. The furniture was faded, the walls bare except for a large, gilt-framed color photograph of a man's turbaned head. The guy had a long brown beard and was smiling serenely. The Swami, of course.

Our host straightened up as if the mere fact of having guests had miraculously rejuvenated him, beamed at us. "Knew who you were all along," he said.

Nigel swiftly held a finger up to his lips, peeled off his backpack, fished out a sensor cube, and cut a circle with it through the air. "Clean," he said.

" 'Course it's clean," Patrick said. "You think I've gone senile?"

"It had," Nigel said, "crossed my mind."

"Gotta be careful out there," Patrick said. "Once you open that door, you're fair game."

We followed him down a dark flight of stairs, into a dirt-floor cellar. Pushing a battered trunk to one side, he felt around in the dirt, found a handle, and pulled open a trap-door. Light came from below. Nigel and I went down a narrow staircase, our host behind us. An alcove led into a book-lined study. Indirect lighting shone from the ceiling. The walls had mahogany paneling. A thick blue and orange carpet covered the entire floor. A bar was over in one corner, a computer terminal and monitor in the other. I couldn't spot the dancing girls, but Patrick looked a bit old for that kind of fun anyway.

"Make yourselves at home," Patrick said.

That was okay with me. I stretched out in a black leather recliner. Nigel chose a padded swivel chair. Patrick brought us drinks, went into the next room and presently returned with a tray of sandwiches.

"Keep them handy," he said, "for guests."

"They let you have guests, eh?"

"Sure do. Long as they're peaceful."

"Peaceful Haven is nothing if not civilized," Nigel said.

"Peaceful, too," Patrick said.

"Certainly," Nigel said. "The only ones who still exercise the more primitive impulses are the security police."

"Make up for those who don't," Patrick said. "Fair's fair."

Nigel introduced us, said, "Patrick was on the scientific board that planned this paradise."

Patrick lowered himself onto the couch, took a pull on his drink. "No need to get testy, Nigel, I was merely taking orders. Scientists don't run this town like in Tech City."

"Seem to've done a thorough job," I said.

"Had plenty of help. Figured out what kind of dope to put in the water, how to dope up the food supply. Simple stuff like that. Can't stop progress. Now everybody's peaceful, just like the Swami wants." He grinned. "Except some folks."

"Always a few troublemakers around," Nigel said.

"Darn right," Patrick said. "Got me a water purifier down here, a food detox lab. Built it while they were fixing up the dope system. Then I took early retirement."

"Early retirement I can understand," I said. "That's one of my ambitions too. What I can't figure is why'd you want to hang around here. Couldn't Nigel get you out?"

Patrick shrugged. " 'Course. In fact, I could've left on my own."

"You *like* it here?" I asked.

"It *is* peaceful," Patrick said. "You gotta admit that. And it's home, isn't it?"

"But everyone's doped up."

"Oh, not everyone," he said. "All of us on the science board have remained unpeaceful."

"Just you guys?"

"Land sakes, boy, haven't you ever heard of women scientists?"

"Uh huh."

"Well, there were plenty of those. And hundreds of others, too."

"Picked the cream of the crop, I suppose."

Patrick shook his head. "More like we picked our friends. What're friends for, right?"

Nigel finished his snack. "You see, Dunjer, there are men of science in many of the more repressive city-states who have elected to stay. They and Tech City form a loose network."

"Why?" I asked.

Nigel shrugged. "We're still working on that."

"But surely," Patrick said, "you gentlemen haven't come all this way merely to chat."

"By spaceball," Nigel said, "is hardly 'all this way.' "

"Perhaps you came to bestow some honor on me?" Patrick said. "It's always been one of my hopes."

"The honor of serving the cause," Nigel said earnestly.

"What cause? That's not much of an honor," Patrick said.

"It will have to do."

"I was hoping for at least a medal."

"Maybe next time."

"At my age there may not be a next time."

"I'll have one sent to you," Nigel said. "If we survive this mission."

"Thank you. I hope you survive. Now what're you boys trying to rope me into?"

"Remember Amanda Splat?" Nigel asked.

Patrick nodded slowly. "That was a ways back."

"Before the Swami," Nigel said.

"So what about her?"

"We need her back."

"Thought you gave her to us for keeps."

"So did we. She's got a talent we can use."

"Talent? Now that's a good one. Only talent she ever showed here was for making trouble."

"She around?" Nigel asked.

" 'Course she's around. Women like that can't get out of here all by her lonesome."

"Know where we can pick her up?"

"Got a pretty good notion." Patrick stretched out his legs, looked at us both. "Woman was trouble from day one. Only a teenager when you brought her, Nigel, but it showed pretty quick. Got into one scrap after another. Simply couldn't live peaceably. Figured when we got around to fixing the water and such, the problem'd be over. Forget it. Something was wrong. Dope never took properly with that woman. Just wasn't peaceable, no matter what. Got a mean streak, I guess, and a peculiar internal chemistry. Can't figure it myself. And if I can't, who can? Think she got meaner as the years went by, too. Yep, guess I know where she is, all right, but I wouldn't count on taking her away with you. Some things just aren't in the cards, Nigel."

"Why not?"

" 'Cause she's in the holding tank at the city jail, that's why."

Nigel sighed. "You sure?"

"Heard about it couple days ago. Wouldn't have even seen the judge by this time."

"Jail her usual residence?" Nigel asked.

"Every Monday and Thursday, seems like."

I said, "Any good lawyers in town?"

Patrick hooted. "Not even bad ones. Police arrest you, it's because you're guilty. Violating the peace. That covers just about everything, see?"

"Yeah. How about pulling some strings?" I asked.

"Used up all my strings getting this," Patrick said, waving a hand at his domicile. "And that was ages ago. Really am retired, you know. Only halfway official duty I still got is inspecting the Dope Works. Drop in from time to time, see that it's up to snuff."

"How often?" I asked.

"Every now and then, whenever the spirit takes me."

"Hmmmm," I said.

"Darned if I like the sound of that," Patrick said.

"They rarely do," I told him.

CHAPTER 20

The Dope Works was at the edge of town. It was still daylight when we turned up there.

"Don't know how you talked me into this," Patrick said. "It's not peaceable."

"You are doing it, Patrick, for the good of humanity," Nigel said, "for the good of your soul—"

"But mostly because it's fun," I said.

"Haven't had fun in years," Patrick said.

"Despite the grave risk," Nigel said.

"Hardly any risk at all," Patrick said.

"No doubt," Nigel said, "what you are doing is an example of your allegiance, nay, devotion to Tech City—"

"Place can go stuff itself," Patrick said.

"Easy on the pep talk," I told Nigel, "he'll want an extra medal."

"I'll settle for money," Patrick said.

The Dope Works was a huge, square concrete structure, surrounded by a high wire fence. I didn't see any guards around. Patrick stopped by the mech-box at the gate, identified himself. A spotter eye scanned him and us.

"Who are the other two?" a metallic voice demanded.

"They come in peace," Patrick told the voice.

The gate swung open soundlessly.

We stepped through, went up a gravel path toward the building.

"Very obedient," I said.

"These mechs," Patrick said, "will take Daddy's word for just about anything."

"That's you, eh?"

"Don't see any other daddies around, do you? Had them programmed special."

"In case the need happened to arise?"

Patrick shrugged. "Never know with that Swami; man isn't dependable."

We halted at the door. The mech-box and Patrick went through their rigmarole again. The door opened.

"Get more gullible each year," our guide said, grinning.

Inside wasn't much better than outside. The place was cavernous, the walls and floors concrete. A huge machine about three stories high took up most of the space. Pipes branched out from it in all directions.

"My baby," Patrick said with some pride. "Hasn't misbehaved yet."

"Always a first time," I said.

We stripped off our backpacks. I removed the long cylinder. It was filled with liquid that Patrick had cooked up in his detox lab. We each had one.

Patrick pointed to one of the pipes. "That's the one, boys. Unscrew the spigot, pour in the juice, and you're all set. Keeps the mischief localized. Won't get the whole town riled up, just some of it."

"That feed into the police station?" I asked.

"Swami's dumb, but not that dumb. They got purifiers."

Patrick, cylinder in hand, started for the pipe.

"What do you have there?" a metallic voice demanded behind us. The voice didn't sound friendly at all.

I turned. Three mechs, out of a storage recess in the right wall, were moving toward us. They were humanoid, but made of black polished metal.

"Friends of yours?" I asked Patrick.

"Never saw them before," he said.

"Your Swami's thrown us a curve," Nigel said.

"He's getting cagey," Patrick said. To the mechs he said, "We come in peace."

The magic word didn't work this time. They kept coming. We began backing up.

"I am Patrick," Patrick said. He waved his arm around. "This is all my doing."

"You are in our memory banks," the lead mech said. "But the other two are unknown to us."

"Friends. Peaceful friends," Patrick said, an ingratiating smile on his bearded face, as though that might actually make a difference to mechs. "I am merely showing them my creation."

"It is not your creation," the mech said. "The water system belongs to the state."

"Surely," Patrick said, "I merely meant—"

"Unauthorized visitors are forbidden. It is the law. What is in the cylinders?"

"It is nothing," Patrick said.

"Give it to us."

"Don't beat around the bush," I said, "do they?"

"I don't think I can control them," Patrick said.

"You're not sure yet?" I asked.

"Well, Dunjer," Nigel said, "security *is* your business."

"Can't deny it," I said.

"So make us secure."

Our backs were almost to the wall. "I was afraid you'd want something hard," I said.

Reaching into my backpack's handy pocket container, I dug out my scrambler cube. "Watch," I said.

"Is that a weapon?" the lead mech demanded.

"Yeah," I said.

"It is useless. We are invulnerable."

"That's good to know," I told it.

"Give—" The mech didn't get any farther. It stiffened,

swayed, and keeled over sideways, like a sack full of rattling silverware. Its two pals, as if delighted at this new trick, instantly followed suit. The racket they made landing on the concrete floor echoed through the vast chamber. The trio twitched for a moment, then lay still.

"Not very dramatic," Nigel said.

"You expect them to scream and bleed?" I asked.

"But satisfying."

"Thanks," I said. "Satisfaction is our motto at Security Plus. This little product of ours I've just demonstrated beats the competition by miles. I'd try to sell you one, but this probably isn't the right time, eh?"

"Probably not," Nigel said.

Patrick nodded at the fallen hardware. "They will be able to identify me."

I returned the scrambler to the backpack, dug out my laser. "Not if I open their repair covers and burn out their think-tanks," I said.

"The mech-box?" Nigel asked.

"I can erase its memory of the last hour," Patrick said.

"You'll still be the first guy they grill," I warned him.

"You shouldn't overestimate the Swami," Patrick said. "However, someone else *could* take the blame, thereby rendering the point moot."

"Someone true-blue," I said, "who just happened to be passing through."

"I think you've hit on it."

"I've had practice."

"Shall we get on with this?" Nigel asked.

"Yeah," I said, "why not?"

Dusk had almost become night in Peaceful Haven when the first signs that 'Peaceful' might not be the right moniker for this burg began turning up.

Some guy ran screaming down mid-block. He hurtled along as if being chased by an army of ghouls.

A large stone was in his hand.

He sent it flying through the window of a clothing store as he galloped by.

A burglar alarm cut loose.

Cops poured out of the station house a block away, tumbling over each other in their rush to get at the guy, as though this might be their last chance to club someone in years. At that, it took 'em a while to down the joe and drag him off.

"Some crazy kid, eh?" I said.

"The power of the people," Nigel said, "is indeed fearsome to behold, Dunjer."

"Just one people," I said. "Not enough to do us much good."

Nigel and I had parked ourselves in a darkened doorway near the symbol of Peaceful Haven repression: the big precinct house in the center of town. We'd ditched the Swami's white robes for more useful attire: black body suits and utility belts.

We waited. It wasn't for long.

Two more customers for the holding tank showed up, screaming their heads off. As though the mere thought of being peaceful another second had driven them berserk. The cops dragged 'em away, too. In between, squads of cops took off on their cycles, bound probably for adjoining blocks. Faint screams from far away reached right into our doorway. Not bad. But not quite what the doctor ordered.

"Patrick's juice takes its own sweet time," I said.

In the shadows next to me, Nigel nodded. "Can't expect them all to get thirsty at the same time, can we?"

"Yeah, but I'd had hopes."

During the next hour, the loonies began to increase. It kept the cops on their toes. But didn't bring the bonanza of mayhem I was looking for. That came some twenty minutes into the second hour. By then, both Nigel and I had started to wonder if the folks in this area would *ever* get thirsty enough to put us in business.

We needn't've worried.

They came in small groups at first, shrieking and yowling their rage. Some thirty cops were now out on the street, taking on all comers. The groups began to merge, become crowds. More cops left the station house, bringing water cannons, clubs, and stun guns with 'em. Cops from other districts had begun cycling in.

The crowds merged again, became one howling mob. The block in front of the station house was thick with frenzied bodies, squirming, twisting, thrashing, slogging it out for all they were worth.

The mob had finally turned into a nice full-scale, uncontrollable riot. About time, too.

Nigel and I swapped glances, moved out of our doorway, and crept away from the tumult. Screamers ran past in knots—men, women, and kids—and paid us no mind: they were being drawn by the cluster of chaos behind us like flies toward a garbage spill.

We turned a corner, doubled back on a street parallel to the one we'd been hiding on. An alley took us to the back of the station house. The sounds of struggle, breaking windows, screaming, and hitting were plainly audible. We had the back of the building all to ourselves. We weren't planning on camping there.

My laser fried the lock off the back door. I pushed it open and we stepped into a dim rear hallway. Empty. Tumult sounded from deeper in the precinct, up front. Nothing new in that, it was all our doing—with help from some locals. We ignored it, took the fire stairs up to the fifth floor. The transient holding tanks, according to Patrick, were on the floors below, reserved for those yet to be processed. Those waiting for a hearing were in the fifth-floor cell complex. Finding Amanda Splat should've been a cinch under ordinary conditions. But things weren't exactly ordinary just now.

I pushed open a door. A narrow corridor led to yet another door, this one locked. A chorus of screams and yells came from behind it. As if the street fracas had found its way up here to welcome us.

My laser made short work of the lock. We entered.

Rows and rows of cells. Half the town seemed to be caged in this lockup. Most of the inmates were still bleeding. Plenty were out cold. A lot were manacled hand and foot.

"Jeez," I said.

Nigel nodded. "Patrick may have overdone it a bit."

"Whadya mean Patrick. Credit where credit is due. Without us, he'd never've thought of it."

"Well, we *are* trying to save the universe."

"Just keep telling yourself that."

We began walking through the narrow aisles between cells. We got lots of attention. Hands reached through the bars, tried to grab us. Voices screeched. Feet pounded on the floor. Shoulders tried to dent the bars. Our presence was inciting this crew—any second they'd wig out again in full force.

"Know what this Splat woman looks like?"

Nigel shrugged. "Your guess, Dunjer, is as good as mine."

"My guess is worthless," I told him.

No profit hanging around here, we couldn't tell one prisoner from the next. We made tracks for the front of the building, hunting for guidance, someone who could lend us a hand. It took a while.

The only authority left on the floor turned out to be a little man in blue uniform, hiding behind a closed door. He sat at a desk with an empty glass and a bottle that looked suspiciously like booze.

He glanced from us to my laser and back again. "Who're you?" he asked.

"Allow me to introduce myself," my companion said with a slight bow. "I am Professor Nigel of Tech City. Perhaps you have heard of me?"

"Uh uh," the guard said. "The Swami don't like us to

hear about no foreign stuff. Didn't even know there *was* a Tech City."

"Take it from me, pal," I said. "There is one."

"Tom Dunjer," Nigel said, "from Happy City."

"Where?"

"Where's not important," I snarled. "What we've done is."

The little guard thought it over. "And what's that?"

I waved at the clamor coming from outside. "All this."

Nigel smiled pleasantly. "My friend and I put a drug in your water supply."

The guard smiled crookedly. "We got plenty drugs in there already."

"Not like ours," Nigel said. "Ours drives people insane."

"Insane?"

"Unpeaceful," I said.

"Yes," Nigel said. "As in the streets."

"Or in your cells, pal."

That was it. We'd done our best to get old Patrick off the hook, short of giving ourselves up to the mercies of local justice. Considering what we'd done here, even that was a thought. Although not a particularly bright one.

"Nigel and Dunjer," Nigel said. "Think you can remember that?"

The guard nodded dumbly. He stared at us. "But why?" he managed to get out. "Why'd you do it?"

"To create a diversion," I said simply. "One that'd get most of the cops out of the station house."

"And then rescue Amanda Splat," Nigel explained. "Take her away from Peaceful Haven."

"*That's* why you did this?"

We both nodded.

"You didn't have to do that," the guard said, all but whining. "We'd a been glad to give her to you, honest."

"Give her to us?" I asked.

"Sure. We've been tryin' to get rid a that dame for years."

We'd never have found her without the guard, even if the holding tanks were empty. She wasn't in one. He took us to a locked metal door at the end of a side corridor.

"She's here so often," the guard said, "she's got her own private cell."

"Just like home, eh?"

"Better," the guard said.

He used a key on a large, jangling key ring, swung the door open.

The room contained a bed, sink, mirror, toilet, old-fashioned TV, small barred window with a frilly pink curtain, and a large, bulky lady dressed in white prison pants and blouse.

"Miss Splat?" Nigel asked.

"What's it to you, bub?"

"It's her, all right," the guard said.

She glared at us. "What do you want?" she demanded.

"To set you free, ma'am," I said.

She put her hands on her ample hips, glowered at us. "And what if I don't want to go?"

"Go, please go," the guard said.

"Madam," Nigel said reasonably, "everyone wants to be free."

"Says who?"

"You won't come with us?" I asked in some wonder.

She made a fist. "Let's see you make me."

Nigel shot her with a stun gun.

I caught her before she hit the floor, almost wrenched my back.

"I had imagined," Nigel said, "that this was going to be the easy part."

"There is no easy part," I told him. To the guard I said, "You got a couple spare cycles and an attachable wagon around here?"

"Yeah. In the subbasement garage."

"This garage have a back way out?"

"Sure."

Nigel and I slung the lady over the guard's back. "Let's go," I told him.

CHAPTER **21**

We made our way through the marketplace. There was plenty of cheap food around in outdoor stalls, wagons, or just laid out on the sidewalks. The small dingy shops behind these displays seemed to carry the same line of goods. Cut-rate garb hung from racks in front of clothing stores. Ancient tenements made a fine backdrop to the whole scene. Clotheslines were stretched between fire escapes. Wash dangled merrily on them, the only merry thing in sight.

Nigel and I wore faded trousers, worn shirts. Our shoes were properly scuffed. Our stint in Peaceful Haven had given us that drawn, tired look that made us almost indistinguishable—we hoped—from the other folks prowling around. There were plenty of them, either hunting or hawking bargains, chintzy nickel-and-dime items. They filled the pavements and cobblestone streets. Some vendors pushed handcarts, others rode horse-drawn wagons. Kids ran underfoot. Beggars held out cups and hands, pleaded for donations. A couple of minstrels had broken into song, their voices thin and reedy like straw.

Off in the distance, the sky was black with smoke, belched from factory chimneys. Even the owners of these sweatshops were said to be dirt-poor by other city-state standards—which was only fitting for a place called Poorsville.

Nigel and I moved slowly, steering Amanda Splat between us. She still wore her wrinkled white prison uniform. No one gave her a second glance despite the fact that she looked like a sleepwalker; she and her outfit fit in perfectly.

"Which way?" I asked.

Splat halted. Glassy eyes failed to take in her new, run-down surroundings. But then we weren't relying on her eyesight. I wasn't sure yet what the hell we *were* relying on. Something that paid off, I hoped.

"Right," she said in a small voice.

Right was more of the same. We slid through the crowd. A magician, shirtsleeves rolled up, was doing card tricks. He had a nice crowd around him. Two guys were selling sausages to the onlookers.

I said, "How long she gonna stay under?"

"Long enough to do the job."

"You sure she's up to it, pal?"

"My dear Dunjer, being sure is my profession."

"Uh huh. Then why's it taking all day?"

"Perhaps," Nigel said, "the snippet of drug I administered is interfering somewhat."

"Some snippet," I said. "From where I sat it looked like a lethal dose."

"You want her wide awake?"

"God forbid."

He shrugged. "It may, of course, be all these people."

"What about 'em?"

"Too many."

"I'll say."

"For *her*, Dunjer."

"Oh."

I halted our human compass again. "Which way, kid?"

She stood still as though listening to some inner voice blabbing away, then nodded slightly to the left. Left it was.

Although it felt more like the runaround to me. We moved.

"Yes, Dunjer, this crowd could be a hindrance."

"It's certainly hindering *us*."

"Or," Nigel said, "she could simply be out of practice."

"If it's simple, how come you don't know?"

"These sisters," he said, "are unique."

A cluster of folks was directly in our path, huddled around a crap game. We made a detour. I stopped Splat again, got her to re-aim us properly. We continued our trek, which seemed to be less productive by the second.

"You see, Dunjer, we never dreamed we might need them someday, or different city-states would have been chosen."

"Like those next door?"

"Who would want them next door?"

"True."

"A city-state with a phone book. Then we could merely look them up."

"No phone books here?"

"No phones. Poorsville, after all."

"Your folks," I said, "just dumped the other sister and went away?"

"She was too old for the orphanage, and too young for the poorhouse. What would you have us do?"

"What about your science network?"

"It does not extend to this place. If they had a scientific complex, they wouldn't be so poor."

"Probably can't afford one."

I stopped our guide yet again and asked the all-important question.

Her mouth opened. Slowly she said one word: "Straight."

That sounded like progress. Almost.

"Hey, mate, she sick?"

It was a little man peering up at us.

"Uh uh," I said.

"Looks kinda green 'round the gills," he said.

"Just under the weather a bit," Nigel explained.

"Should take her to the tent hospital, mate."

"No need," Nigel said. "We're taking care of her."

"Check 'er over, mate, don't take no chances. Remember the plague."

"Plague?" a fat woman barked.

"Plague?" a beggar cried. "Plague?"

Heads were starting to turn.

"What about the plague?" a skinny man demanded, glancing from us to Shorty.

"This fellow here," Nigel said, nodding toward the small man, "thinks he may have the plague."

"I do not!" he bawled.

"But he's too shy to admit it," Nigel said sweetly.

Nigel and I propelled our charge forward, away from the hubbub that had suddenly congealed around the little guy. The crush opened and closed behind us.

We kept going.

"What's this about a plague?" I asked.

"Lord knows. Places called Poorsville usually have plagues. You *are* vaccinated?"

"Yeah, if the plague turns out to be the measles. Which way?" I asked Splat.

"Straight."

"Boy, I hate this," I said.

The woman suddenly dug her heels in.

"There, there," she murmured.

"Where there?"

I could feel her stiffen against my arm. I followed her gaze.

The crowd here had thinned out a bit. Sitting on the curb was a skinny dame with a wicker basket full of brightly colored shawls. Her brow was furrowed, cheeks sunken, nose like a beak. She was scowling at nothing in particular, as if trying to hone her favorite expression to a fine line.

"How come I don't wanna go over?" I asked Nigel. "I who have faced a thousand dangers?"

"Because you're a sensible chap, Dunjer."

"How about just yellow?"

"That, too."

I tried to move Amanda forward, but she'd taken root like a small stubborn tree. I couldn't budge her. Her eyes, still glassy, were fixed on her sister. Something besides Nigel's tranquilizer was working on her.

"Come on, Dunjer, before someone says plague again."

"I'm game. Our pal here's having second thoughts."

"Even first thoughts," Nigel said, "are quite beyond her at the moment."

"Tell her, not me. I'm just the escort service."

Nigel turned, eyed her closely. "Strange."

"Yeah, along with everything else here. Grab her arm, pal, and lift."

He nodded. We grabbed, lifted, and hauled. A job better suited for mechs. But who ever heard of mechs in Poorsville?

Again we were attracting attention. A couple of nearby folks were staring at us. "One of her fits," Nigel said loudly. "Nothing catching."

"Let's hope," I muttered.

The sister noticed us, too, after a moment; we were hard to miss. She jumped up from the curb as if she'd been sitting on an open flame.

"Heyyyy," she wailed. "What is this?"

We lifted Amanda off the ground and covered the last few feet in record time. A real act of desperation.

"Gretta Splat?" Nigel asked breathlessly, a winning smile on his face.

"Nice won't work here," I whispered.

"Get her away from me!" Gretta spat.

"See?" I said.

"We'd like to take you home, Gretta," Nigel said gently.

"She don't know from nice," I said.

"Home?" she barked.

"Surely," Nigel said, "poverty can hold few attractions. Come with us and—"

"I ain't goin' with HER!" she screeched.

"Gotta use muscle," I told him. "No way around it."

"Your sister's presence, my dear, is only temporary. Let me assure you—"

"Be gone, be gone," she hissed, waving her arms as though making a spell. She was starting to back up.

"Madam—" Nigel began.

"We're gonna lose her, pal."

I glanced around. A tattered juggler was performing with a bunch of balls a couple of yards away. A crowd had gathered around him, with more headed in his direction. An old lady was selling apples, another cookies. No one was taking any notice of us anymore.

I slipped the stun gun out of a back pocket. Keeping it low at my hip, between Amanda and me, I tried to block the stunner from prying eyes.

"I'll scream!" Gretta shrieked. "Go! Go!"

I fed her a charge.

She had almost backed up to a storefront. She stiffened, fell against the plate-glass window, and slid down to the pavement like a deflated balloon.

I stood very still, looked around. If anyone had noticed our little sideshow, they weren't doing much about it. The juggler, adding one ball in the air after another, was holding his audience spellbound.

Nigel and I propped Amanda up against the wall next to her sister. I put the basket of shawls at their feet.

"Nice family portrait," I said.

He looked at them sourly. "What do we do now," he asked, "wait until dark and carry them off piggyback?"

"It's a thought," I said. "But maybe I've got a better one. Got anything we could use for dough here?"

"Actually, I do." He stuck a hand into his pants pocket, removed a wallet, rummaged in it, and came up with a wad of brown paper notes. "Poorsville currency."

"The real McCoy?"

"Collected by our Tech City Department of Native Affairs. Those of us who go on field trips make a habit of carrying native money. If nothing else, it keeps one out of vagrants' prison. It's also good for buying a snack, should the need arise. Or even a native artifact."

"Or renting one." I took the wad of bills and made my way through the crowd. The old guy with the horse-drawn fruit-and-vegetable wagon was where I'd last seen him. He turned a fast thumbs-down on the notion of letting me rent his rig. Till he got an eyeful of what I was offering. Probably a king's ransom in these parts. But I figured the Tech City Department of Native Affairs could afford it.

The wagon, with me perched next to the driver, moved at a snail's pace through the crowd. When we reached our trio, I hopped off and helped the prof load the two sisters aboard. We got the usual crowd of busybodies around us. Maybe the wagon made us look respectable, if not exactly official. No one raised any eyebrows.

We sat next to the driver—the Splat sisters sacked out on the edibles—and made our way slowly out of town.

CHAPTER **22**

"Yes, my dear Dunjer, there is a reason I have saved this city-state for last."

"Scenic wonders?"

"Hardly."

"Lemme guess," I said. "It's the toughest, meanest, rottenest, most loathsome one we've come to yet. The one we're sure not to get out of alive."

"On the contrary," Nigel said. "The reason I have saved the Great Kingdom for last is that it's the easiest."

"I've heard that one before."

We were strolling down a dirt road, trees and fields on both sides of us. We could see a few spires sticking up over the next hill. We were dressed in ordinary clothes for once, a pleasant enough change.

"Must have phone books in this burg—right?—if nothing else."

He nodded. "Along with other conveniences. A modern kingdom, it's claimed—whatever *that* means."

"It's really great?"

"Few things are, least of all kingdoms—unless, of course, the King himself can be so classified."

"And in this place?"

"We'll just have to see, now won't we?"

There was plenty of activity in town, people racing around as if being nipped at by invisible bugs. I had no intention of asking them why. I was afraid they might tell me.

"Energetic citizens," I said.

"Subjects," Nigel said.

"Either way," I said, "just watching 'em run around makes me tired. Still, they seem to have a neat kingdom here. After those other rotten city-states, this place doesn't look half bad."

The shops were all painted mint green. Trees were planted in earthen squares on the sidewalks. There were benches every few feet. The roadway was wide and clean and the few cars that wheeled by looked classy.

"Yeah," I said. "You've got to hand it to 'em. On the surface, everything's just peachy. And the surface is just where I want to leave things. No need to poke around here, ask a lot of dumb questions, stir things up. All we gotta do is go into some store, and look this dame up in the good old phone book. Once we know where she hangs out, it should be no big deal to kidnap her. We've had plenty of practice."

Nigel nodded.

"Yeah, it's painless," I said. "Except for the victim."

"It *is* difficult to imagine one of the Splat sisters as a victim."

"Maybe. But that was before we came along."

We went into a drugstore. The pay phone was right next to the door, and directly underneath, in its very own niche, the Great Kingdom phone book.

"Clean streets, phone books, I bet the buses even run on time," I said admiringly. "All we have to worry about is this dame having married and changed her name."

"Who in their right mind would marry one of the Splat sisters?"

"You've got a point, Prof. What's her first name?"

"Helga."

"Okay." I opened the phone book, turned to S, ran my thumb down the page and studied my find.

"Only one Splat listed," I said.

"And?"

"It's Helga, all right."

Nigel beamed at me. "A breeze, as they say."

"They may say it, but that doesn't make it so."

"Doesn't?"

"Uh uh."

"May I ask why, Dunjer?"

"Sure. The word before 'Helga' is 'Queen.' "

He hesitated. "As in Royal Highness?"

"They don't mean Lowness, pal. And she isn't hawking shawls on street corners either. Her address is the Royal Palace."

"Well now," the woman said, "this *is* a most enlightened monarchy and I could *almost* say that old King Gustove had a couple of bats loose in his belfry, but not *quite*. You understand?" She shot us a piercing glance.

Both Nigel and I nodded in unison, as if our understanding was as well-developed as the biceps of Mr. Happy City himself, which were bigger than the guy's noodle.

We were out on the street chatting with a middle-aged, round-faced, redheaded lady who was seated in a small wooden booth labeled VISITOR INFORMATION.

"I would certainly hesitate to even *think* that he was utterly, hopelessly deranged," she said, "let alone say it. Especially to strangers."

"We didn't hear a word," I said. "The King married Miss Splat?"

"He did, alas. It was one of the poor man's last acts. Soon's he passed on, the Queen changed her name back to Splat. Said it had a nicer ring to it."

"Rings like a broken alarm clock," I said.

"Where did you gentlemen say you came from again?"

We told her.

"Well, one place's as good as another."

"Visitors from *any* place are kind of unusual," I pointed out, "in most city-states."

"Here, too," she said, "when the King was alive."

"Miss Splat," Nigel said, "encourages tourism?"

"Indeed, yes."

"After the bucks?" I said.

"More like the tourists. So they can hear her speak."

"She speaks to tourists?"

"To everyone. Once a day. Twice on Sundays."

Nigel nodded thoughtfully. "Draws a nice crowd, I suppose, being the Queen and all."

"Every last man, woman, and child in town."

"Must be some speaker," I said.

"A few would say she just prattles on," the woman said. "Not I, of course."

"So how come they all show up?"

"Attendance is compulsory. That's why," she said, "everybody's in such a rush. You see, they're trying to beat the deadline, finish their business before she begins."

"And when is that, my dear?" Nigel asked.

"In another hour, at the Great Kingdom stadium."

"Sounds like we shouldn't miss it," Nigel said.

"You can't. It's compulsory for tourists too."

Nigel peered through the spaceball porthole.

"Yes," he said, "the spaceball comes equipped with many useful devices, for you must remember, my dear Dunjer, that its primary function is archaeological study. And once in the wilds there is no telling what frightful monstrosities will have to be pacified. I myself have encountered in my travels the many-taloned zruff, the nail-toothed sly, the winged kratch, not to mention the wild natives of Leech, who proved to be the most dangerous and cunning of all. I bought their homeland for twenty-eight colored beads, the best, I might add, that the Tech City dime store had to offer. But then, the shiftless swine went back on their solemn pledge and demanded more. In fact, they shamelessly held out for one hundred and twelve beads. When I patiently explained that in the civilized community, a deal is a deal, and I had only brought those twenty-eight, they became quite belligerent. It was all I could do to escape with my life. I would not be at the controls of this spaceball now if I had not made use of one of its many very useful features.''

''Which one?'' I asked, gazing down at the world below. ''The fast-takeoff button, the magnetic door seals, the high-intensity floodlights?''

Nigel shook his head. ''No, Dunjer, none of those. I used the spaceball cannon and blasted them to smithereens.''

I looked at the guy. ''You kidding?''

''Yes. What do you take me for, a homicidal maniac?''

''I gotta answer that?''

''We in Tech City would never resort to violence—unless it was absolutely *very* important and profitable. The Queen should be well into her speech by now, wouldn't you think?''

''Uh huh.''

''Well, down we go.''

The spaceball began its descent.

''What're you gonna do, bomb 'em?''

''I am going to do what I did in Lower Lixzax when a roaming herd of snout-faced grinx made landing impossible. I will release a tranquilizer gas over the stadium which will render the occupants utterly docile. Then while I hover, you will descend a rope ladder and bring Queen Splat aboard.''

''And if this doesn't work?''

''*Then* we bomb them. But have no fear, Dunjer, the snout-faced grinx were a very lively bunch, far more lively than subjects of the Great Kingdom. There is nothing to worry about.''

* * *

I kicked the guard in the guts; he doubled over. He was being docile now, but not as docile as the prof had promised.

A soldier drew his laser. I rolled out of the way as a laser blast burned a hole where my feet had been.

A second guard came at me. I used the stun gun, sent him reeling.

I ducked behind the lectern, peered out through the goggles of my gas mask. About twenty uniformed guards and soldiers, scattered through the stadium, all in gas masks, peered back at me. The rest of the crowd—including her Royal Highness—was out for the count.

The rest of the crowd didn't matter. I and my fellow gas-maskers were the only players in this game, a game I wasn't apt to win.

A laser beam took a bite out of the lectern.

I made myself small on the floor, or as small as a guy my size can make himself, grabbed Queen Splat by the shoulder, and yanked her over. She was a short, plump lady with a round head and pert features, an improvement over her two sisters, but nothing to brag about.

My back was to a wall. I was safe from that direction. That left every other direction to worry about. I got an arm around the Queen's waist and hauled her up, half-propping her against the lectern.

The troops were closing in.

I gave 'em a peek at their leader.

"Freeze," I bawled as though I were being backed by an armed riot squad. "One move and she gets it!"

That stopped them in their tracks.

Now all I had to do was figure out what "gets it" meant. I looked around.

The spaceball was overhead, rope ladder dangling down within easy reach. But there was no way I could get on it without making myself a perfect target.

The wall behind me was a makeshift affair with a stage door over to my right stuck in it—for theatricals, no doubt.

That gave me a brainstorm.

I got my arm all the way around the Queen's waist, as if a bit of hanky-panky in this tight spot would be just the ticket. Crouching behind her, I began backing sideways like a crab, toward the door. I held the laser to her head as though I were plugging a leak.

"She gets it," I shouted, "if anyone moves—see?"

I still hadn't figured out what "gets it" was. The troops probably had their own ideas, because they kept a low profile.

I inched over to the door, put my back against it and felt it give.

"Stay where you are," I yelled over the Queen's shoulder. "Anyone comes through this door, she's a goner!"

With a little luck I was going to be a goner too.

I stepped through the doorway, kicked the door shut behind me.

For a moment I had cover. A moment was all I needed.

I craned my neck skyward.

Nigel didn't need any encouragement. The spaceball had followed my progress, was directly overhead, its ladder lowered to the ground.

I tossed the Queen over my shoulder, and nearly fell down. I grabbed the ladder with both hands, keeping her Highness pinned between it and me. The spaceball moved up and away.

We were out of gun range in an eye blink. I began climbing the ladder with Splat tucked over my shoulder like a sack of onions. Slow going wasn't the word for it. My hunch had been right: nothing was going to be easy in this mess.

CHAPTER 23

"Ugly, ugly!" Gretta yowled, her thin, bony face distorted by rage. She was glaring at her two sisters.

"Shaddup, you bitch!" Amanda screeched, balling her fist and gritting her teeth.

"Decamp from our presence *at once!*" Helga demanded, trembling, her round face white and pinched.

"I'm sure they would if they could," I told Helga, "but since they can't, they won't. That goes for you too, sweetheart."

"How dare you address our person in that manner?" Helga shrilled.

I gave her a hard gaze. "Yeah," I admitted, " 'sweetheart' doesn't seem to fit."

"I am her Majesty, the Royal Highness!" Helga howled.

"Scum!" Gretta spat.

"Filth!" Amanda hissed.

"Uh uh," I told Helga. "Not that either. Maybe back in the Great Kingdom you were top dog, but here you're just one of the plebes."

"How dare you!"

"Practice," I said. "Practice has made me a regular daredevil."

"When I get loose," Amanda raged, jaw muscles bulging, fingers writhing, "first them, then you!"

"That's *if* you get loose, kid. Let's be precise."

Nigel shook his head. "Doesn't seem very likely, does it?"

"Not very," I agreed.

The three Splat sisters were seated in straight-backed armchairs, their wrists manacled to the chairs. Amanda was on one side of the small metal-walled room, Gretta on the other, and Helga in between. We hadn't bothered tying their feet to the chair legs, and we didn't want them close enough to kick at each other.

"You *are* giving sisterhood a bad name," Nigel said.

"We should keep you here just for that," I said. "But we've got a better reason."

"Lack of cooperation," Nigel said.

"Yeah," I said, "that's it, all right: the better reason."

Amanda squirmed in her chair. "Bastards! I'll belt ya black and blue, tear ya limb from limb—"

"May your innards rot," Gretta intoned in a singsong voice, "your noses become leprous, your fingers twisted and palsied."

"My dear Dunjer," Nigel said, "you seem to fit that description already."

"Merely wishful thinking, Nigel old thing," I said. "You know what they say about sticks and stones."

"Our person cannot abide this!" Helga wailed. "Not a moment longer, not an instant."

"Well," I said, "practice *does* make perfect, just like I said. After a couple years you'll get used to this little windowless cell, and even each other."

"And, my dears," Nigel assured them, "you will certainly become accustomed to the utility mechs we shall station here, to make sure you don't wiggle out of your chairs somehow and get into mischief."

"You can't do that!" Amanda shouted.

"But we have," Nigel said.

"Look, buster, I've been in Peaceful Haven lockups hundreds of times. I know my rights!"

Nigel beamed at her. "That was Peaceful Haven. Here in Tech City you have no rights. In fact, no one except us even knows you're here."

"Think of it this way," I said. "The three of you'll really get to know each other."

"If not at first," Nigel said good-naturedly, "then in the years to come."

"Or maybe decades," I said. "True friendship takes time."

In the silence that followed, the three dames tried to stare us to death. It didn't quite work. We waited.

Helga was the first to speak. "What do you want?"

"Ah," Nigel said, "reason and logic have triumphed. How nice."

"Not so fast," I told him. "That's just one out of three."

"Dear me, I do believe you're right."

Another silence followed. I broke it.

"Well?" I said.

Slowly, as if her neck had ossified, Amanda nodded once.

"I'll see you in hell for this," Gretta told us.

"Is that an affirmative?" Nigel asked.

"Yes," she mumbled.

"Bravo!" he said. "I knew you lovely ladies wouldn't let us down."

The three sisters glowered daggers at him.

"I see I have your attention," he said. "That is most important, as this is a very delicate matter. We know of your collective powers and we wish to make use of them."

"How?" Helga demanded.

"You will guide us through Time-Warp Valley."

I looked at the guy. Time-Warp Valley. The site of the M-bomb explosion a century ago. There were no guideposts there, no landmarks, just a lot of funny-looking vegetation. But if you went through it, you could find that you'd lost or gained days, weeks, months, or even years. The M-bomb had screwed up everything, including time.

"So that's what this is about," I said to Nigel.

"Of course. How else are we to obtain an activator? You ladies will remain here, under mech guard, but psychically, acting as one, you will guide us through Time-Warp Valley so that we emerge three years ago."

"Never!" Helga yelped.

"I won't work with them!" Gretta shrieked.

"Count me out," Amanda bawled. "I hate 'em!"

"And they hate you, my dear," Nigel said, "but you shouldn't let a thing like that stand in the way of a far greater, nobler objective—namely your release. Help us now and you can each go your separate ways. I believe you already know the alternative."

Again there was a silence. I folded my arms. Nigel leaned back against the wall. We didn't have long to wait this time. Three heads bobbed reluctantly, as if being tugged by invisible strings.

Nigel said, "Once we have laid our hands on the specific item we seek—something you ladies need not concern yourselves with—you will guide us back across Time-Warp Valley to the present time. And then into the specter worlds."

CHAPTER 24

"Right! Right!" the voice shrieked. It sounded like Gretta, but who could be sure? The voice was rattling around in my noggin like loose debris in a high wind.

"Up! Up!" a second voice shrilled. Amanda probably.

"Down, you fools, down!" the third voice chimed in, making the confusion complete. They sounded like boozed-up Happy City traffic cops before the mechs took over.

I turned to Nigel. "Well, at least they're psychic."

"But not complete," he said.

"They're giving me a headache."

"The Splat sisters' revenge," Nigel said.

Down below was Time-Warp Valley. The nutty vegetation, the pink hills beyond. It rang a bell, all right. I'd been through it once before with no major mess-ups. But this time we had to pinpoint our destination, get it down to the yard. So far, our guidance team had laid an egg.

Nigel flipped a switch. "What are they doing?" he asked.

"Sitting in a circle, squabbling," a metallic voice answered back.

"Tell them," Nigel said, "that it is back to the cell and chairs if we don't have results immediately."

"I do not believe they like each other," the metallic voice intoned.

"Leave the speculation to me," the prof said. "Just give them my message and appear menacing."

"Won't have any trouble with that last bit," I said. "What do you use that thing for?"

"Sews clothing. Those appendages do look a fright, don't they?"

"Yeah, let's hope our ditsy sisters have a good enough imagination."

The voice was cool, precise, and very feminine. "Take your ship down," it said, "and follow my instructions implicitly."

We'd been hovering up above the valley, out of potential harm's way. Now we floated down. Nigel and I swapped glances. The girl sounded worth knowing.

"Merely a psychic projection, Dunjer."

"I was gonna ask for her phone number," I complained.

"Trace that voice back to its origins," Nigel said, "and you have the Splat sisters. I'd be delighted to fix you up with any one of them."

"Death first," I said with simple dignity.

"Gentlemen," the voice said, "do you see that row of twisted trees due south?"

"Uh huh," I said.

"Fly directly over them."

"Aye aye," Nigel said.

"At my word turn northeast."

"Northeast," Nigel said.

"Now."

We turned.

"Continue in this direction at your present speed for another eighty-one seconds, gentlemen. Then skim over that cluster of treetops."

I looked down through the porthole. Lush vegetation blossomed below. I couldn't tell one shrub from another. The

M-bomb had meshed them all together. The trees looked like they'd been kneaded into long, ropelike strands. The place gave me the creeps.

"Now head west, across the stream," the voice said. "When I give the word, reverse course. Maintain the same altitude and head directly for those blue hills behind you. Now!"

"Now" it was. The spaceball turned.

"Good. When you emerge from the valley you will be three years in the past. I believe you can find your way back to Happy City on your own?"

"Yeah, we just might manage that," I said.

"I shall guide you back through Time-Warp Valley when you are ready."

"Uh huh."

"And I would be glad to give either of you gentlemen my phone number, if I had one—"

"Not having one," I said, "is a distinct drawback."

"Not having a body, my dear Dunjer, is even worse," Nigel said.

"Although the detective," the voice said, "is already spoken for."

"That's security op," I said, "not detective."

"How did you know that?" Nigel said to the voice.

"You *did* ask for a psychic?"

Nigel parked the spaceball in a wheat field on the outskirts of Happy City and we waited for nightfall.

"What happens if I meet myself?" I asked.

"Don't even think it," he said.

"That bad, eh?"

"Worse. I don't believe I could stand two of you."

"Aside from that, pal."

"Do you remember meeting yourself three years ago, Dunjer?"

"Uh uh."

"Then you didn't."

"But if I did?"

He shrugged. "Hypothetically, it could no doubt change things. History might be scrambled in ways we cannot even begin to imagine."

"Maybe for the better."

"And perhaps not. You don't really want to meet yourself, do you?"

"Two would be better than one," I pointed out.

"And three would be one each for the Splat sisters."

"How about we forget the whole thing?"

Happy City looked pretty much as I remembered it. It took me a moment to realize that some things *were* different. The top three stories were back on City Hall. The Qerk building, which had been torn down last year, was still standing tall. Mom and Junior's Eat Palace hadn't gone all mech yet, and the food was still lousy. You'd think at least one of the two humies would've known how to cook.

Laura was around somewhere in town. Not with me, because we weren't an item yet. I missed her. I was here too, grabbing forty winks by now. For two cents, I'd've sent my younger, fresher self off on this job. Only, knowing me, I was sure I wouldn't go.

Our first stop was the Sass abode.

The house was dark, its inhabitants snoozing away. I used the override cube to short the alarm system, and opened the front door. We made a beeline for the back of the house—the doc's workroom.

"Watch your step," I told Nigel.

A butler mech was stretched out on the floor.

"A peculiar place to sleep," Nigel said. "If mechs slept."

"Part of the security system," I said. "Cube puts 'em out like a light. It'll be as good as new in a while, which for these old-time mechs is nothing to write home about."

I went directly to the painting on the wall, removed it. The safe was there as I knew it'd be, having been here before; although before was yet to come. I didn't waste time thinking about it. Again I used my cube. The safe door swung open.

Three prototype activators lay inside. I stuck my hand in, pulled out one of the the small gadgets that vaguely resembled a hand-held, miniature entertainment system: dials, bulbs, a tiny screen, something that looked like a bottle opener but probably wasn't.

I gave our prize to the prof. ''It's your baby, pal, handle with care.''

''If I can't, who can?''

''Sass, for one. Only if we wake him now, it'll shake up history like a malted milk, right?''

''Waking that grumpy little person,'' Nigel said, ''Would be even worse. We'd never hear the end of it.''

''Yeah, he ain't a sunbeam like us.''

I closed the safe, we retraced our steps down the long hall and out the front door.

I reversed the cube, turning the security system and butler back on.

We made tracks.

Linzeteum was the fuel that powered an activator. It was stashed in the Security Plus safety vault, in the subbasement of the World's Emporium, directly across from the Security Plus building. At this hour it seemed safe enough for Nigel and me to hop an underground chute, connect with an interoffice chute, and be conveyed there in style. We hopped.

The final stretch—through a long corridor—we walked.

''Yes,'' I explained to Nigel, ''the safety vault is impregnable. There's absolutely no way anyone can get in there. Except, someone once did, and now we're doing it again. Although we're doing it before it was done last time. And for the very same product, no less. Of course, I'm authorized to use the vault at will. But not to remove products that belong to clients. On the other hand, think what's at stake here. Actually, I'm not even sure what's at stake anymore. I don't know why I'm even doing this. I hope there's a good reason, but aside from Laura, I'm starting to have my doubts. I suppose that's reason enough. But what I'd really like to do is begin this week all over again and do it right. But, of course, that would louse up history. So here I am breaking into my own safety vault. What irony, eh? Better me than a stranger, I suppose. Am I making myself perfectly clear?''

"You are jabbering at me, Dunjer."

"Yeah, I was wondering what I was doing."

We rounded a bend in the no-frills, white-walled corridor.

"Hi, boss," XX21 said.

"Golly," I said. "I'd forgotten *you* were on duty here."

"Boss, you should take care of yourself. Your brain must need a good tune-up, maybe even a complete rewiring. I'm *always* on duty here."

"You won't be in a couple of years."

"Not the demolition chamber, boss, not that! After years of selfless, devoted service—as though I had a choice."

"Actually, I was thinking of a promotion."

"A promotion? Gee, boss, you really *must* be sick. And now that my eye cells focus on you properly, I can see the signs of incipient illness all too plainly. The bags under your eyes, the lines in your face, the slight unseemly stoop. As though you hadn't slept in weeks."

I went to the safety vault. "Just a couple of days, XX21."

"Boss, you look ten years older!"

"There years! Not ten, just three!"

The spotter eye gave me the once-over, the scanner scanned my thumbprint, the X-ray device greeted my skeleton like an old friend. The large door swung open. I stepped in, went to the Sass safe, had my thumbprint scanned again. The safe door opened.

The linzeteum was nestling in its cubical. I reached in, yanked it out.

"Got it," I said, swinging the door securely shut again. After all, it was my vault.

"Boss," XX21 said, "what have you got there?"

"Linzeteum."

"Should you be taking it?"

"Of course not."

I handed my find to Nigel.

"Who's he, boss?"

"My accomplice in crime."

"You *are* going to return it?"

"Sure. What's left of it. When're we bringing this almost useless product back?" I asked the prof.

"Before night's out."

"Short crime spree," I told the mech.

"Oh, dear," XX21 said. "This certainly taxes my loyalty circuits. As guardian of the safety vaults, I must allow no unauthorized withdrawals. But as your employee, I must obey your every instruction. Good thing you mentioned promotion, boss, or I'd really be in a tizzy."

"You are in a tizzy. There are times," I said to Nigel, "when I'm not sure the setup here's foolproof. But I can't put my finger on the weak link."

"It will come to you," Nigel said, pocketing the product.

CHAPTER **25**

The Splat sisters were pretty much as we'd left 'em.
 They were seated in overstuffed easy chairs on the
fortieth floor of the Science Complex Building in the heart
of Tech City. Their eyes were closed as though they were
taking a simple noonday nap. The sewing mech was over
by the door, for all I knew dreaming about stitching shirts
and trousers. A couple more mechs were on the other side
of the door. Four windows looked out over the city, but the
Splats would've needed wings to make a getaway through
them. Between the sewing mech, the other guards, and the
high floor, we had the Splat sisters sewn up tight.
 "What do we do," I asked, "wake 'em?"
 "They are merely the untidy parts. We must speak to the
glorious whole."
 "The doll."
 "The voice."
 "As she pointed out, I'm already spoken for."
 "Well, I'm not."
 "Welcome back, gentlemen," the voice said.
 "You got a name, kid?" I asked.
 "You may call me Talps."
 "C'mon," I said, "that's 'Splat' backwards."

"I prefer it to 'kid.' "

"Haven't you got a name of your own?"

Nigel shook his head. "Remember, she is merely a pro-jection of the three sisters, Dunjer; she has no independent existence of her own."

"Sounds like a bundle of laughs."

"We each have our burdens to bear. Mine appears to be you. Talps," Nigel said, "can you guide us to the specter worlds?"

"What is it you seek there?"

He told her.

"Yes, it is within my power to guide you."

Nigel gave me a smile. "The question, you see, was just rhetorical. I'm quite familiar with their abilities."

The voice was icy. "Not *theirs* but *hers*. They have no abilities. Nor will it be that simple a task to find the specter world you want among the many others. All are offshoots of the continuum worlds, which are stable; the specter worlds are not. This makes everything more difficult."

"Like always," I said. "We know all that, Talps."

"Then you know how daunting the task is. As I speak to you now I have no idea where this specific world you seek might be. But the goods which were transported from our world to it left their marks in the fabric of the universe. Once these tracks have been found, I can guide you along them."

Nigel nodded. "I will need a short while," he said, "to construct a temporary activator shield."

"How long?" the voice asked.

"An hour or two at most," Nigel said. "The blueprints are among my papers. I developed the concept years ago, you know."

"She does now," I said. "We wake the sisters?"

"Allow them to slumber," the voice said. "It will be less vexing for everyone."

"For a voice," I said, "she's got a head on her shoul-ders."

* * *

It was a good four hours before the prof finished tinkering in his lab and we were ready to move.

This time around we hoofed it to the airfield. I wanted to take an outdoor gander at the Tech City skyline before heading for trouble.

The prof and I were dressed mostly in black: slacks, flex-shoes, and deep-pocket zipper jackets. My shirt was midnight blue, which might just as well have been black. Now all we had to do was turn up on this specter world in the dead of night and we'd be all but invisible.

"I've had the spaceball outfitted with a whole arsenal of weapons," Nigel said. "Defensive as well as offensive. It will give our enemies pause. Perhaps we will be able to reason with them."

"Yeah, if they've got any brains, which, considering what they've been up to, is doubtful. You got the shield squared away, right? No slipups, no catastrophes in the making, nothing I should worry myself sick over? Let's hear it, Prof; the last time I went on a little trip like this, I almost didn't make it back."

"It is in place. In theory the shield will, for a while, hold back whatever catastrophe the fates might launch at us."

"That 'for a while' part doesn't sound so hot," I said. "Actually, I'm not too keen about 'in theory' either."

"The shield," Nigel said as we entered the airfield, "may be quite unnecessary."

"You dig doom?" I asked him.

"You are speaking of the continuum worlds, Dunjer, those known as Interworld. But our probable destination is one of the specter worlds. The activator should have no ill effect on its shadowy, insubstantial existence."

"And if we don't end up on one of 'em?"

"Then, my dear Dunjer, we apply the most stringent of all scientific principles, namely we keep our fingers crossed."

* * *

"You are ready?" the voice asked.

"As ready as ever," Nigel said.

"There will be no need to fly the spaceball," Talps said. "Merely turn on your activator, do not set a course. I shall act as your compass and guide you through the fabric of the universe."

"Sounds simple," Nigel said.

"Nothing's simple," I said.

"Now," Talps said.

CHAPTER 26

We stood on a street corner.

Traffic in front of us was bumper-to-bumper— horns blared, motors whirred, coughed, and sighed as if the mere thought of one more spin was too much to bear. The air was thick with exhaust fumes. An unending stream of people clogged the sidewalk. Tall, dirty buildings around us bit large chunks out of the gray sky.

"I think we lost something," I said.

"What makes you say that, Dunjer?"

"It's drafty out here."

"So it is."

"The spaceball wasn't drafty."

"Good thinking, Dunjer."

"Thanks, pal, I'm glad one of us is keeping cool. It ain't me either."

"We scientists," Nigel said, "have learned to take small setbacks in stride."

"Small setbacks. Right. Maybe she's sending us in shifts, eh?"

"First us, then it?"

"Yeah."

"Why should she do that?"

"Who the hell knows? This can't even be our specter world," I complained. "Judging by all this traffic, they already got more hardware here than a body can stand. But you're not sweating up a storm, are you, Prof? Come on, what gives?"

He shrugged. "Talps may not have been able to handle us and the spaceball at the same time. Remember, this has never been attempted before. There is, however, no reason to panic."

"I must be missing something, some small, minor point that being in this rotten, noisy crush has driven from my befuddled mind. Go on, Prof, set me straight."

"You forget this." Nigel held up the activator, beamed at me. "*It*, not her, is the source of *our* power."

"Hmmmm," I said thoughtfully. "Darned if I didn't forget the little thingamawhosis. My mind *has* clogged up. Let's blow, pal, before this messy place really gets me."

He nodded. "Our best course is to return to Tech City."

"Sure, I'm kind of homesick myself. Although, actually, we've only been gone some five minutes."

"Calm yourself, Dunjer. We must return to find out what has happened to the spaceball, to harness it to us by activator power. That spaceball will be invaluable when we reach our specter world."

"When, eh? What I like about you is your endless, cheery optimism. Note I didn't say mindless. Let her rip."

Nigel peered at the tiny screen, turned a dial, glanced up at me, nodded once, and pressed a button.

"Well?" I said.

"I may have been wrong, Dunjer."

"About what?"

"Perhaps it *is* time to panic."

"Hell, Prof," I said, "it's *always* time to panic in my racket. Welcome to the club."

"It may have been tampered with." Nigel had the back cover off the activator. "See here?"

All I saw was a lot of circuits and wires.

"A small jump-switch has shorted out," he said.

"Don't look at me; I wouldn't know a jump-switch from a do-hinky."

"How is it possible?"

"Bad education?"

"Not that, Dunjer. I mean how could anyone tamper with this?"

"For a while," I pointed out, "the activator was in your studio and we were in your lab, remember?"

He nodded. "But who would know to do such a thing?"

"Maybe the guys who've been plundering Happy City."

"Then we were being watched, all along."

"Could be. Or maybe your jump-switch was defective to begin with and just blew on its own."

"It is not *my* jump-switch, but Sass's. He would test all parts before assembling them. I think."

"That's the catch, all right: excessive thought. This thing could've happened on its own, right?"

"I suppose so."

"So what's a jump-switch?"

"It triggers the jump from one world to the next. Obviously. Sideways as it were."

"Yeah, obviously."

"These are alternate worlds, Dunjer; time on them is the same, but events are different."

"We stuck here?"

"Given the proper equipment, I could reconstruct this part. But on this world . . ." He shrugged. "I wouldn't even know where to begin to look. And time is important."

"Some anthropologist," I said.

"Gentleman anthropologist. My field is hard science. You, Dunjer, are the security expert. This should be more in your line."

The traffic light changed from red to green. A crush of pedestrians poured across the street, many of them shoving their way into the building behind us. A clock, high on a tower, said 5:10. I glanced at the street signs: Lexington Avenue and Forty-second Street. Uh uh. I turned my gaze east, saw part of a familiar glass and metal structure.

"Nigel," I said, "see that large building behind us. It's called Grand Central Station. We're in New York City. The glass tower over toward the east is the U.N. building."

"I'm flabbergasted. You know this awful place?"

"Yeah, unfortunately. I call this the U.N. world. You find it, you get to name it. Though the people here found it first. Sass and I were through this world once, on the tail of a guy who'd swiped an activator and was touring Interworld. We didn't catch up with him in time and this whole city was flattened by an H-bomb. Place might've reverted to normal after we left; we weren't here to check up on it."

"Seems perfectly fine now," Nigel said. "Which is more than can be said for us."

"Us may be finer than you think, Prof."

"You are truly demented, Dunjer."

"Sure, but aside from that I've got an idea. It's really your idea, Nigel, but *I* thought of it in *this* world."

We didn't have far to go, just a few doors down.

"Yeah," I said, "there're plenty of similarities on these worlds." I waved my hand. "Note this drugstore."

"This is no time even to consider drugs," Nigel said stiffly.

"Uh huh. Just come along."

The floor of the store was cluttered, full of all kinds of sundries except drugs, which were hidden behind a counter.

I found what I was looking for over by the wall.

"See there," I said. "A telephone. And right underneath, a pair of phone books."

"You wish to call someone on this blighted world?"

"Yeah, the rescue wagon, only there isn't one. The phone books are what I'm after."

"What do you hope to find there?"

"You never know, Prof."

* * *

"You see, Nigel," I said, "Talps must've gotten us from Tech City to Happy City and *then* over to this world, before she and/or the activator conked out."

"How could you possibly know *that?*"

"It was a snap to figure," I said modestly, "once I realized I'd been here before. An activator jumping from world to world more or less leaves you in the same spot on each one, right? And the last time I was here, I'd come directly from Happy City. Naturally, lots of things are going to be different because these *are* alternate worlds. But some things are gonna be the same."

"You are stealing my thunder, Dunjer."

"Just some practical knowledge I picked up along the way, Prof. That was the last time I had to save the universe. You'd think the universe would've learned to look out for itself by now."

"Are we almost there?"

I stopped under a street lamp, fished out the map I'd swiped off the drugstore rack. "Almost."

"You said that twenty minutes ago."

"This is more almost. Have faith, pal: the map wouldn't lie, even if I would."

We were hiking along lower Broadway according to the map. Soon we'd reach Canal.

"We could, you know, have gone in style," Nigel said irritably. "I have a pouch full of jewels, gold coins, and worthless beads just for such occasions."

"The natives here have worthless beads of their own," I said. "You'd've had to change the other stuff into local currency. And that could've led to a lotta questions. This way's simpler. Besides, the exercise will do you good."

"Exercise is one thing," Nigel said. "Trudging along these alien streets is something else again."

Some ten minutes later we hit Canal.

"Trudge right, pal," I said. "It's just a hop and skip from here. I'd add jump, but with the activator on the blink, there won't be any jumping, will there?"

We headed west, toward a stretch of water the map called the Hudson. Both cars and pedestrians had thinned out. The street was lined with darkened storefronts that, according to the signs, sold all kinds of cut-rate goods during daylight hours: clothing, appliances, electronic supplies. Most of the stores were shuttered tight, as if trying to ward off the darkness.

"You still refuse to tell me where we're going?" Nigel demanded.

"You didn't fill me in on why we needed the Splat sisters, remember? So this is a surprise," I said. "What kinda surprise would it be if I spilled the beans now? Let's just say it's a little touch of home on a distant world."

"You've become insufferable, Dunjer. Some of these stores might very well have equipment we could use. Have you thought of that?"

"Yeah."

"We would have to break in, of course."

"Of course. But I've got a better place to burglarize."

It was one of the last buildings on the street, all the way over on Canal's west side. Only a highway and the water lay beyond it. The six-story, yellow brick structure took up an entire block. It looked new.

The sign over the front door read SASS ELECTRONICS.

The windows were dark, the neighborhood almost deserted.

Nigel turned from the sign to me. "You knew this?"

"How could I? What I did was look in the yellow pages under electronics. Those yellow pages are a sure sign of a top-heavy advanced society with plenty of items to sell. Like electronic supplies that you could use in patching up our activator. I just ran my thumb down the S's, on a hunch sort of, and there was old Sass."

Nigel looked dumfounded. "He sells electronics on this world?"

"Manufactures them," I said. "Probably invents 'em

too. Guy even had an extra ad in the phone book. Seemed like the natural place to visit, no?''

We used the back door.

The security system was too primitive for the override cube, but the scrambler cube—which scrambles almost anything—worked just fine. I made sure by monitoring the system with my monitor cube. There was no inspiration cube. I still had to do my own thinking. Too bad, I could've used a breather after all that hiking. ''So much for delicacy,'' I said to Nigel, frying the lock with my laser.

A shoulder to the door popped it open.

We moved silently through the darkened ground floor, our flashes lighting the way. Just offices, file cabinets, computers that looked as though they came out of the dark ages by comparison with their Happy City nephews.

''Looks like the old boy's doing okay,'' I said.

Nigel shrugged. ''There was always a materialistic side to his character.''

''Can't all be saints like us,'' I pointed out.

We didn't use the elevator. A wide, carpeted staircase took us to the second and third floors. More of the same.

''Must have a strong union,'' I whispered. ''Everyone's gone home.''

''Then why are we whispering?''

''First thing they teach you in private eye school. Always whisper when you're breaking the law.''

''What happens if they catch us?''

''The loony bin if we give 'em the straight goods, the pokey if we don't.''

''Are you sure, Dunjer, that they *manufacture* their goods here?''

''I'm not sure of anything,'' I said.

We didn't bother exploring each floor. As soon as we caught sight of the offices, we turned tail and headed for the next landing.

We hit pay dirt of a sort on the fourth floor: workbenches,

tools, all kinds of parts stored away on shelves, in storage rooms. I trailed behind the prof as he wandered through the hall.

"Well?" I asked.

"Perhaps," he said. "Let's see what's upstairs."

The fifth floor had more workbenches, but the hardware looked different even to my untrained eye. Nigel didn't bother making the grand tour, but merely beamed his flash over the equipment. He shook his head. "Top floor," he said.

He perked up as soon as we got there.

The layout was more spacious here, the space divided into expensive-looking laboratories. Nigel dashed off to peek into each one, me tagging along at his heels like a vestigial tail. We stopped in the largest one of all. By now the prof was smiling.

"They appear to be behind us scientifically in many ways, Dunjer, but in some ways, I wouldn't be at all surprised if they were a smidgen ahead."

"That covers it every which way," I said. "Except the most important one. We in business, Prof?"

He nodded. "We'll have to risk using these bench lamps. And it may take me some time to find out what they actually have here. But yes, I think we *are* in business."

The prof started for a supply room.

A voice behind us said, "Nigel! Dunjer!"

We both turned.

"What in heaven's name are you doing here?" the voice from the doorway demanded.

It was Dr. Sass.

Gone was the toga. The little person with the bald head, round face, Vandyke beard, and tufts of white hair behind each ear was dressed up in a gray pin-striped three-piece suit. A white shirt, red, blue, and gold tie, and pointy, highly polished black shoes rounded out his attire. He carried a briefcase and rolled umbrella. He peered at us intently.

"Why is it dark in here?" He reached out a hand, flicked on the lights. "There, that's better." His eyes widened as he took us in. "What are you doing in those outlandish costumes? Jogging outfits, are they not? Keeping fit, I see." He wagged his head. "All to the good, certainly. Would do it myself if I had more time. And burning the midnight oil on some project again, eh, Dr. Nigel? Dragooned Mr. Dunjer away from his duties to assist you, I see." He beamed at us paternally. "Well, far be it for me to complain. I have, as you know, always applauded such initiative. And if you need Mr. Dunjer, that's fine, too." He thumped the wall with a small, round fist. "This building is secure enough as it is. Nothing to steal in any case. Try not to work all night, Dr. Nigel." He beamed at us, waved his briefcase, turned on his heel, and was gone.

Nigel and I both stared at the empty doorway.

"I didn't imagine that, did I?" I asked.

"Who," he said, "could possibly imagine a thing like *that?* I couldn't get a word in edgewise."

"Just as well, pal, you didn't want an extended powwow with the guy."

"He's not the Sass I know."

I shrugged. "He may actually be a better example of the genre. Who knows?"

"We work for him, Dunjer."

"Yeah, or all hell would've broken loose. Don't look so stricken, Prof, nothing wrong with making an honest living."

"Perhaps on some other world *he* works for *me?*"

"Or maybe both you guys work for me mopping floors."

"What a ghastly thought."

I sat peering out the window while Nigel worked on the jump-switch. Lights twinkled from tall buildings in the distance and from smaller ones nearby. I wondered what was going on in some of those buildings. My last jaunt with an activator had been like a roller coaster ride. No time to really take in the sights, get to know the natives. With disaster nipping at my heels, it was all I could do to keep one jump ahead of it. Only now it turns out the natives are me and the rest of the gang. Or at least some of 'em. That changed things, but not necessarily for the better. I wasn't any too tickled about working for Sass, myself. I wondered if I'd connected with Laura on this world, and what she did here. I even wondered if crime was as enterprising here as in Happy City or if the natives had somehow managed to beat the odds.

I looked over at Nigel at the workbench.

"How's it going?" I asked.

He gave me something that could have been a nod.

I went back to gazing out the window and wondering if I was the type of guy I'd admire on this world. I wondered about the rest of the human ops in Security Plus and if any of them had hit the jackpot here. I even wondered if Mayor Strapper was a big-shot politico here or just some paper-pushing civil servant, or something entirely different, like maybe the head of a corporation. I was starting to depress myself when my wondering was cut short by a noise in the hall. Sass coming back for another look-see?

I got up, strolled to the door, and peeked out in the direction of the stairs.

"Over here, sir," a voice said from the other direction. I turned.

Dr. Cyrus Spelville stood in the hallway. He wore a gray jacket, red bow tie, and black trousers. He was as rotund as ever—but why should the Spelville of this world have gone on a diet? The first surprise was that he was somehow tied up with Sass here. The second was that he held a very large gun in his chubby hand.

Every once in a while it's time for a bluff, and this looked like the time. "Come off it, Spelville!" I barked. "Put away the heater before someone gets hurt. I work here, pal. Take a close look, it's me, Dunjer, in these running duds!"

"I know very well who you are, sir." His belly shook and three chins jiggled as he spoke.

"So what's with the gat?"

"The only damn way to restrain you, Dunjer," another voice said from behind me.

I looked over my shoulder and there stood Chief Constable Krimshaw.

The chief was wearing his CHIEF insignia cap. He had on a dark blue shirt with the inscription KRIMSHAW SERVES THE LAW. His pistol belt was strapped around his bulging belly, but the gun was in his hand. I recognized that gun. It was a laser special, regulation firearm for the Happy City cops.

"You guys have come a long way," I heard myself say.

"The least we could do for a fellow worlder," Spelville said. "Kindly raise your hands."

CHAPTER 27

I raised 'em.

The three of us stood in a dim circle of light that spilled out from the lab. The rest of the floor was a puddle of darkness.

"Can't keep out of trouble, can you, Dunjer?" Krimshaw said, a note of sadness in his voice.

"Trouble's my business," I said. "It says so on my calling card."

"You could've gotten along without *this* trouble," he told me.

"Look who's talking," I said bitterly. "Spelville I can understand, he's a crook by nature—"

"And years of backbreaking study," Spelville said. "One must perfect one's little gifts."

"But you, Krimshaw," I went on, "were sitting pretty. You had your job and all those perks too. Why do you need this?"

"For more, Dunjer, that's why. Besides, I still have my job and all those perks."

"Shame on you, Krimshaw," I said. "You sold out, worked hand and glove with the bad guys, covered for 'em, bled Happy City dry—"

"You're wrong, Dunjer, it was wet as ever the last time I looked, which was just eight minutes ago. Sure, I took my cut—comes with the job. But I've been straight with you, Dunjer. What would I do with City Hall or a factory full of parts?"

"What would anyone?"

"There you have it. All I'm here for is to take you back to Happy City."

"Precisely," Spelville said. "You and your meddlesome companion. If he wishes to avoid bloodshed—namely yours, sir—he will come out at once with his hands high in the air."

"Bloodshed? Now, hang on, Spelville—" Krimshaw began.

"We are not here to pussyfoot," Spelville barked. "We have our instructions."

"You guys shouldn't be here at all," another voice called out from somewhere behind me.

Too many voices, that was for sure—the only sure thing in this mess. And all of 'em equipped with disagreeable bodies that had hands holding guns. I turned my head in the direction of this new voice, looked to see who we were dealing with now.

"Jeez," the voice said from the darkness.

I couldn't see a thing, but the voice sounded familiar. Another Happy City cohort. A couple more and we could have a party, then go on a tour.

A large flash appeared in the constable's hand, its beam cutting through the dark. Krimshaw thought he was still back on home turf. "Come out, you!" he boomed.

Tom Dunjer, dressed in the sappy brown uniform and peaked cap of a night watchman or doorman, crouched behind the banister of the main staircase, a gun in his hand.

Krimshaw and Spelville gawked at him. They weren't the only ones.

The moment's diversion produced results. The light flicked out inside the lab.

My foot sent Krimshaw's flash spinning off down the hallway. It clattered somewhere against the wall.

Darkness.

I didn't wait for an invitation. I ducked, dived into the lab, and kept rolling.

Nigel slammed the door behind me. A lock clicked into place.

Shots sounded from the hallway. By then I had my laser out. Someone had to warn my other self about laser guns, what they could do.

Nigel grabbed my arm. "This way," he hissed.

"Uh uh. We Dunjers gotta stick together."

"Don't be a fool, there is more at stake here than the life of one man."

Another shot sounded.

"You mean the damn universe?"

"I mean two men—*us!*"

"That *is* a thought," I began.

The burglar alarm cut me short. It seemed to be coming from all sides, as if the walls themselves were outraged at our presence here. This had to be Dunjer's work—so at least he was still alive. If the cops knew their business on this world, they'd be here in minutes. Taking the heat off the other Dunjer.

"Come," Nigel whispered, yanking at my sleeve.

I didn't argue. Once the heat was off my other self, it'd be right back on me and the prof.

I moved, followed Nigel across the darkened lab floor.

Behind us the door banged open. A laser blast had no doubt cooked the lock. I crisscrossed the doorway with my laser beam, gave them something to think about, a bit of on-the-spot education. Education makes perfect, but these guys were too far gone for that, I figured.

Nigel shoved me through another doorway. A second door led us back into the darkened hall, a good distance from the lab. No one was there.

We tiptoed away from the staircase, serenaded by the

alarm, which sounded glad for the workout, more than could be said for me. A supply room was Nigel's destination, one with a metal door. We stepped in. He turned the lock, flicked on the light. The room was small, its shelves, stretching from floor to ceiling, covered with equipment. I didn't see any side exit or back door, a real drawback to total peace of mind.

"What do we do," I asked, "camp here for the duration?"

"That would be very inconvenient."

"Yeah, not to mention short."

He squinted at the open-backed activator, seated himself on the floor, stuck his hand into a deep pocket, and pulled out some tools he'd pinched from the lab. Taking hold of a small soldering iron, he plugged it into an outlet and got busy.

A couple of minutes dragged by. The room was getting stuffy.

"Another moment back there," Nigel said, "and we would have been ready to leave, I believe."

"You gotta show me, Prof, I'm a skeptic."

"Patience, Dunjer."

"Come out," a voice called, "with your hands behind your heads. I hear you in there."

The other Dunjer. The guy got around.

"He hears us," I said. "We Dunjers're tough to fool."

Maybe he'd have gotten a raise, I thought, if he'd nabbed the lot of us. Now he'd have to explain to his boss and the cops why one of the thieves looked like his twin brother. Unless Nigel screwed up. Then we'd all get to chat about it together.

"Make it easy on yourselves," the other Dunjer was saying. "There's no way out."

I fought back the urge to pop a question or two at him about his life here. An extended confab with my other self would do neither of us much good at the moment.

"How you doing, Prof?"

He peered closely at his handiwork. "I think I may have it, Dunjer."

"He *thinks*. Make sure. There're no repair shops out in the fabric."

"Who are you?" the other Dunjer asked, his voice low against the door.

I could hear other voices down the hall, growing louder. The coppers paying their respects. They'd made good time. I wondered if Spelville and Krimshaw were still hanging around, waiting for a last crack at us.

"I'm you, pal," I told the door. "But hopefully much evolved."

"Eh?"

"On the other hand," I said, "who knows?"

Nigel turned a dial. The activator began to click; a couple of colored lights blinked on. If it got up and danced next, I'd feed it a quarter. Nigel peered at the screen.

I could hear a murmured conference on the other side of the door. I didn't have to guess what it was about.

Nigel said, "The monitor shows activity. An activator is in use."

"Open up in there," a new voice demanded.

"Our pals beat it?"

He nodded. "There is a clear path away from this world."

"Open up or we'll come in and get you!"

"Somehow I don't see that pair learning how to use an activator," I said. "You never know, of course."

"Peculiar power source," Nigel said. "Seems to be coming from somewhere off-screen."

"Or even being entrusted with one," I added.

"It does seem unlikely," Nigel said.

"I'll count to three," the cop hollered. "One!"

"That guy's getting on my nerves," I said.

"Give yourselves up!" the other Dunjer called. "Why make trouble?"

"Guy's a philosopher," I said.

"Two!"

"Hey, Prof, don't you think—"
"I certainly do. Hold onto your hat, Dunjer."
"I don't have a hat," I pointed out.
The lab vanished.

CHAPTER **28**

We were spinning head over heels through swirling fog. Below us on the ground tall buildings grew out of the mist, ballooned and shrank like living things whose life processes had been speeded up a thousand-fold. Rooftops, domes, spires reached for us like hands, tried to grab us, pull us down toward them.

We kept spinning.

Lightning singed our heels, thunder deafened our ears. Wind gusts wailed around us like mad, trapped things, tossed us through the sky as lightly as if we were a pair of dried, withered leaves.

"What the hell's happening?" I managed to bawl over the tumult.

"I don't know," Nigel yelled back. I could hardly hear him in the uproar.

"I thought you knew everything?"

"Only in theory."

"Do something, pal."

"What?"

"Anything!"

He turned a dial on the activator.

We were following a short, stocky man through valleys, up hills, across long stretches of plains.

We moved at breakneck speed, helter-skelter through the changing terrain. The distance between us never varied.

Everything was gray. Mist, fog, and a lowering slate-gray sky made the landscape seem a dead, desiccated place.

I managed to turn my head toward Nigel. It took some doing; gravity seemed to have other ideas. "This isn't much of an improvement," I shouted.

"We are in the wake of the other activator," he yelled.

"Who's our pal up front?"

As if in answer, the short man paused for an instant, turned to face us.

We stared at each other. The short man was Dunjer.

"What the hell is this?" I yelled at Nigel.

"We are in a specter world."

"Help me!" the short Dunjer cried. "Help me!"

"Cripes!" I yelped at Nigel. "Press the damn panic button!"

He twisted a dial.

I was in a crowded city. Tall, square buildings rose on both sides of the street. I could see a tall, lean man up ahead. I wanted to reach him for some reason, but the crowd was too dense. I pushed and shoved, my clothing damp with sweat. I used elbows, knees, and feet. I could get no closer to the man up front.

I glimpsed faces that seemed vaguely familiar, as if a crowd of Happy City denizens had been randomly transported to this world. And subtly changed.

A hand grabbed me by the shoulder, shook me.

"Dunjer," Nigel shouted, "they are specters."

The tall man turned then.

It was Dunjer, of course. His thin, elongated face bore an expression of utter despair.

Nigel moved a dial.

We were on a side street in a gray city. I knew the fat figure up the block was Dunjer. He turned a corner. I began to run as though my feet had developed a will of their own. Nigel was behind me. I swung around the corner, saw the fat man far up the street. Small shacks, storefronts, street lamps, vacant lots were all the company he had.

"Wait!" I yelled. Lord knows why. Maybe to chitchat about losing some weight.

The fat man turned. "Save me!" the Dunjer bellowed. "For God's sake, save me!"

"Jeez," I said, stunned.

Nigel was at my side. "The activator has congealed its power around you, is seeking out your specter selves."

"How do we make it stop?"

He spun the dial.

Something that half-resembled the U.N. building and the Happy City City Hall was directly ahead.

The building was gray. So were the small, squat houses leading up to it like an honor guard.

Only one other person in sight. I didn't have to think twice about who this was. He was pushing through the revolving door of the giant building.

I only glimpsed his back, but this Dunjer seemed almost normal. Maybe stooped a bit, perhaps a little unsteady on his feet. But who wouldn't be on a world like this?

This time I really *did* want to talk to the guy, find out what was going on here first hand.

"Come on," I heard myself say, "let's nab him. All this 'Save me' junk needs some going into."

"Do not be taken in by appearances," Nigel yelled. "It is all ephemeral."

"Hell," I yelled back, "those other Dunjers seem real enough. And they're hurting."

I got to the building, not remembering covering any ground. The door revolved behind me. I was in a deserted lobby. Dim light shone through gray windows. Dust covered floors, walls, ceiling. The other Dunjer was nowhere in sight. I saw footprints in the gray dust, followed them around a corner of the lobby, found another door, flung it open.

Stairs receded into the darkness below.

"Dunjer!" I called.

No answer.

I ran down the stairs three at a time into the darkness.

"You mustn't become embroiled in this world," Nigel hollered behind me. "It could prove fatal."

"I'll take my chances," I shouted.

The stairs became a dark tunnel. Smaller tunnels branched off from the larger one.

I ran straight ahead.

A shimmering door beckoned in the distance, glowed with a green-grayish light.

I dived through it, pulled up short.

The other Dunjer stood facing me, not three feet away. I saw now that his hair was white, his eyes sunken, his face lined. This Dunjer was a very old man.

"What's going on here?" I demanded. "What's happened to you?"

The ancient relic of a Dunjer opened his mouth, revealing toothless gums. A dry tongue snaked out over cracked lips. "I've changed," he croaked, "changed . . ."

I stared at him.

Something terrible was happening to the Dunjer. He began to grow taller, thinner, to shoot upward toward the ceiling. "Help me," he whispered. "Help me leave this place."

I could understand his desire. It was one I shared.

"How?" I asked.

He didn't answer, probably couldn't. This Dunjer was strung out like a piece of string. He became a very thin thread. He became nothing.

I heard Nigel's voice behind me. "I think we've seen enough," he said.

"No, wait."

For the first time I looked around, took in the room.

A giant computer lined all the walls.

I found myself moving toward it, my eyes still searching for the other Dunjer.

I stood in front of the computer, punched out a question: *"What has happened here?"*

A strip of paper scrambled through a slot:

Aborted reality.

As if to prove its point, the computer seemed to shudder. A thin crack split walls and floors. I heard a low rumbling beneath me; the building rocked back and forth like a toddler's crib.

"Go! Go!" I shrieked at Nigel.

The dial rotated.

We were back in the gray storm high over the shifting buildings. Lightning crackled and snapped around us. The wind blew but didn't touch us. This time we hung there— stationary, as if suspended by invisible strings, shielded by some unbreakable glass bubble.

Nigel peered at the activator in his hand, a thin smile forming under his mustache. "I think I'm getting the hang of this," he said.

"You had me worried, pal. We ever getting out of here?"

"Oh, yes. The specter worlds, you know, merely are offshoots of the alternate worlds."

"Merely," I said.

He nodded. "The latter is solid, while the former, as we have seen, is quite insubstantial."

"So?"

"A twist of the dial," he said, "could release us from the unpleasant specters, but then we would lose the trail of our two friends which winds directly through these so-called worlds."

"Yeah," I said, "I get it. Unfortunately."

"Of course you do. Since they've taken a route through the specter worlds, it is an excellent bet they are headed for one. Perhaps the very specter world we seek. It would stand to reason."

"Reason has nothing to do with these goofy worlds," I complained.

"They are in upheaval, Dunjer, to a far greater extent than I would have suspected. The passage of an activator from Interworld may have unbalanced them even more."

"They've almost unbalanced *me*. We gotta go through this rigmarole all over again?"

"I think not. I can speed up the process. I have no idea what that would be like, however. Are you game?"

"Yeah. Anything's better than all those screwed-up Dunjers."

"You're quite sure?"

"Fire away, Prof."

The dial revolved.

The storm vanished.

I was being shuffled like a deck of cards, flipped through graying worlds as if a magician were doing tricks for some gigantic celestial audience. Too fast to note anything but changes of light and shape.

The show went on forever. Or maybe just a few seconds.

It stopped.

CHAPTER 29

The shell smashed through the outer wall, showering us in a spray of debris, kept going and tore through an office wall behind us.

By then Nigel and I were on the floor.

We weren't the only ones.

Laura, Mayor Strapper, and a couple dozen vice mayors, deputy directors, and staff were hugging the ground, huddling behind each other and pieces of office furniture. Spelville and Krimshaw were there too, hiding behind the mayor's desk, both looking terrified.

I'd found the top three floors of the City Hall. Or maybe *it* had found me.

Another shell burst through. The outer wall was more holes than wall, I saw. We'd landed in the middle of some kind of war. Just what the doctor ordered after my nice, restful jaunt through the dumb worlds filled with Dunjers.

I crawled over to Laura, got behind her overturned leather chair, and planted a king-size smooch on her lips.

She grabbed me as if I were some kind of surefire life preserver, hung on, as if my mere presence made us all shellproof. "Thomas, I knew you'd rescue me, you crazy kid you."

"Yeah, all I need now is for someone to rescue *me*. What is all this?"

"It ain't fun and games, boss."

"We are under attack, sir," Spelville called out from behind the desk. "You must take us back to Happy City." There was a note of frenzy in his voice.

"I must, eh?"

"This is no time for bickering," Krimshaw called. "We go back a long way, Dunjer, get me out of here!"

"What happened to your activator, guys?" I asked.

"Our *what?*" Spelville demanded.

Another shell whistled through the wall, this one over on the other side of the room. Mayor Strapper, who'd been waving frantically in my direction, ducked.

Nigel wormed his way over to me, small bits and pieces of wall clinging to him like dandruff. "They had no activator, Dunjer, don't you see? That's why the power source didn't register on my monitor. They were being manipulated from afar, reeled in, as it were. The activator must be somewhere *here*."

"That's nutty," I said. "Who'd hang around here, when an activator could take 'em somewhere else?"

"*She* would, Thomas," Laura sputtered angrily.

"She?"

"The woman who runs this place." Laura waved an arm. "All this is hers."

"All *what*, the top three floors of City Hall?"

"Everything, I think. This whole world, maybe."

"Someone," Nigel said, "would seem to be disputing that."

"Where is this dame?" I asked Laura.

"She ran out when the shooting began. To take command of her forces, she said."

"*Her* forces. So where're *our* forces, the mechs that were with you?"

"They went with her, Thomas, to defend us all. She said it was our only chance."

"Jeez, who's she fighting?"

"I don't know."

A couple of shells whizzed by outside, missing our three floors entirely.

"Whoever they are," I said, "they're not very good."

"Good enough to get us all killed, Dunjer," Krimshaw wailed. "Quit stalling and do something!"

"I demand that you return us to our world at once!" Spelville yelled.

"They're right," Mayor Strapper said. He'd crawled over to join our party. "We stay here much longer, we'll never be able to patch up the top floors. Think of the taxpayers if not us."

"We can't just beat it," I pointed out, the merest trace of an anxious whine in my voice. "Not without the other activator. Happy City'd still be up for grabs."

"More is at stake than crime in Happy City," Nigel said. "The activator in use here is unshielded. All of the alternate worlds could be at risk."

"What's he talking about, Dunjer?" Krimshaw boomed.

"The terrible things that happen when an activator is used," I explained simply.

"Terrible things *are* happening," Laura said.

"Not terrible enough," I said.

"Just give them a chance," Mayor Strapper said.

"Uh uh, this is just a skirmish by comparison. When I say terrible—"

Laura put her hand on my arm. "Listen," she said.

I cocked an ear. "You mean all that screaming and shouting that sounds like a thousand cats having their throats cut?"

"That's what I mean."

I stood up.

"You're indispensable, Dunjer!" Strapper shouted. "Watch out for the shells!"

I nodded at Nigel. "*He's* indispensable, I'm just the sidekick. Anyway, the shelling seems to've stopped."

I strode to the window. The glass had conveniently been shot away. I stuck my head out. One look was all I needed.

"Nigel!" I bawled.

The prof was at my side in an instant, leaning out the window.

"Good Lord!" he murmured.

Behind me I heard our crowd scrambling to its feet. Laura and Strapper were suddenly on either side of me, giving me the old squeeze. Spelville and the constable were at another window. All the vice mayors, deputies, and functionaries had taken up posts at holes, windows, and giant cracks in the wall.

What they saw brought a stunned silence to the bunch.

A ragtag army was charging toward us over a barren plain. They carried an assortment of makeshift weapons that ranged from clubs, cutlasses, and muskets to modern projectile weapons. I saw only a couple of lasers. A couple was bad enough. What was far worse were the soldiers themselves. I knew some of these guys, a few were even bosom buddies. But not in their current guises. There was Nigel on a tall, thin body. Only he had three heads. They were all Nigels. Some of the other bodies weren't so lucky. One had Spelville and Strapper sharing shoulders, another, Laura and a vice mayor. Krimshaw's head was stuck on something that could've been *my* body. My head bobbed disgustingly on a number of other shoulders in combination with other heads. The crazed mixtures seemed endless. They were mostly from Happy City, but the Splat sisters were there too, on all kinds of bodies, both male and female.

Our Security Plus mechs, alongside a bunch of other mechs, were stretched in a thin defensive line in front of our building, nobly prepared to do battle.

I turned to Laura. "How many shooter mechs we got out there?"

"One, I think."

"Great."

The line of mechs opened fire, a steady barrage. Multi-heads began to topple. Some turned tail, only to be trampled by the rest. Most kept coming.

"Plenty of shooters," I said. "Where'd she get 'em?"

"I don't know, Thomas."

"Maybe I do," I said. "Remember the mech plant that vanished? What it made was mechs."

Nigel said, "I need some room."

"The view doesn't get any better," I told him, stepping aside.

He aimed the activator out the window. Multi-heads began vanishing in twos and threes, popping out of the landscape.

"Into the fabric, eh?"

"Of course. The heads will be able to keep each other company out there—if they don't implode."

"Short war," I said.

"You are wrong," an imperious voice said. "The waves of multi-heads can be endless. Give me that activator."

I turned.

She was maybe seven feet tall. Her hair jet-black, her features perfect, if somewhat haughty. She wore a long, regal purple gown. One hand rested on her hip, the other held an activator.

I'd never laid eyes on her before, but I knew that voice.

"Talps," I said.

"That is a ridiculous name," she said.

"Not my idea," I reminded her.

"It is, in any case, *Queen* Talps!"

"Uh huh. I've heard that one before, Queenie."

" 'Queenie' is as odious as 'kid.' "

"Sorry. Nice kingdom you've got here."

"It would be, if it weren't for the multi-heads. Give me the activator. I need it!"

"Don't we all."

Nigel looked over his shoulder, said, "I can easily create a force field, my dear, that will fully protect this activator and my friends. But then I will be unable to continue eliminating these pesky multi-heads. You wouldn't want that."

"I could do it myself," she wailed, "if I had more lin-zeteum."

"Running low, eh?" I said.

"It is all but gone."

"You could've saved some, Queenie, if you hadn't sent those two clowns after us."

"Watch that, Dunjer," Krimshaw roared. "There are libel laws."

"Not on this world, pal."

"I did not send them after *you*," she said, "but after the activator."

"Why not bring us directly here then?"

"I did not want you to meddle."

"Meddle?" I said. "We're saving your neck."

The door burst open. Laura screamed. So did everyone else, me included. It seemed the natural thing to do.

Multi-heads poured through. The heads slobbered, grimaced, and drooled. "Kill! Kill! Kill!" they chorused.

Lots of folks didn't know what they wanted. But these lads and lassies did—they wanted to kill.

Only one had a pistol. My laser took him out of play. I burned a Spelville head off a pair of narrow shoulders. Knocked off two heads I didn't know. Laura was still screaming. I saw why. My laser fried a Laura head off a Krimshaw body. My hand was starting to shake. Over by the door a Dunjer head was squeezing through the crush.

"Nigel!" I roared.

The prof had already swung his activator around. "There is no reason to panic, Dunjer," he said. "The resemblance is only skin-deep, I think."

The multi-heads, mercifully, began to wink out.

"Laura," I said.

"Later, boss, I'm busy having hysterics."

"Who's the chief mech down there?"

"XX38."

I stuck my head out the window, bellowed, "XX38,

check behind you! They're getting in here!''

A mech gazed up at me, saluted. I didn't hear the ''Aye aye, skipper,'' but I knew he'd said it. It gave me that deep-down feeling of stability I'd been missing lately.

A squad of mechs took off for the back side of the building.

Nigel kept the activator trained on the doorway. Multi-heads were charging through—and blinking out. They didn't seem to learn. Abruptly, the flood shrank to a trickle and dried up.

''Gone,'' I said, ''for now at least.'' My hands were still shaking. I wondered if they'd ever stop.

''Seems to be slackening off outside too,'' Nigel said, peeking out the window.

''They will be back,'' Talps said.

Spelville cried, ''I recognize the voice, sir!''

''Eh?''

''It was she, sir, *she* whose voice came to me, told me how I might obtain vast sums of money—in return for a few paltry favors. I admit it, sir, I was paid handsomely for my services. But not enough for *this*.''

''Dunjer, for heaven's sake,'' Strapper yelled. ''I appeal to you as your mayor. We must leave here, at once.''

''Damn right!'' Krimshaw shouted. ''As your constable, I *order* you to get snapping, boy. This place ain't safe.''

Laura was pulling at my sleeve. ''That goes for me too, boss.''

The whole crowd was up in arms, roaring, shouting, cursing. It didn't take a mind reader to figure out what they wanted.

I held up my hands. ''Easy does it,'' I said. ''I'm con-vinced. Who wouldn't be?'' To Talps I said, ''This is a real chummy place to be queen and all that, and there're lots of heads to talk to. But Krimshaw's right: it's not safe here. I suggest you return to Happy City with us.''

''That is impossible,'' she said. ''I can exist only on this plane.''

"This plane? Where the hell are we anyway?"

"Well beyond the fabric of the universe," Talps said.

"So we are," Nigel said in some wonder, glancing at the monitor.

I shrugged. "If you want to stay here, Talps, that's your lookout. But all the rest of us are heading home."

"You are a fool," she said. "Their activators have created a tunnel through space-time directly from here to Happy City. What is to prevent them from using it?"

"Them?" I said.

"The multi-heads. They are specter spillovers, created on the specter worlds from you and all these who came in contact with an activator. But not in their present forms. The specter worlds distort. But these spillovers are grotesque! And wicked. They could not exist long on your world, but they would do horrible damage before they perished."

"How," I asked, "did they get that way?"

"When they were pulled off their specter worlds and wrenched beyond the fabric itself."

"By whom?" Nigel asked, flabbergasted.

"My awful sisters, that's who. Specter replicas exist on many specter worlds in infinite variations, as you well know."

"Too well," I told her.

"On one such world," she said, "my sisters possessed *independent* psychic powers. Just as I, three years ago, was able to snare an activator when it was tossed into the fabric by your Dr. Sass, so were they able to land its equivalent. The bond that ties me to the sisters on earth also ties me to the specter sisters. They *knew* that I found a real world, was slowly building it up, and challenged me for its control. Their specter activators were weak or I should long ago have succumbed. But if their activators are not seized, your world will never be safe, they will continue to pilfer. The war here will spread everywhere like a contagion."

I said, "You're saying your *sisters* were lifting all those tools?"

"I and they both. But my efforts at first were peaceful. I needed machinery to create my own mechanized society. I could not take from you indefinitely, for my meager linzeteum supply would not allow it."

"You could've swiped more from the safety vault," I pointed out.

"I did not know of its existence until you showed me."

"I'm glad there's something you don't know," I said. "Your sisters in the same boat?"

"Yes. They stole less than I, for their activators could not handle the load. But their intentions, unlike mine, were never peaceful."

"And just who are you, my dear?" Nigel asked.

"I also was a specter. But my psychic powers were *strong*. I could reach out to earth, to beyond the fabric itself to find this world. I used the activator to achieve solidity. It is only just that I should rule here."

The shelling had begun again. But the multi-heads' aim was worse than ever. Their tussle with our mechs and Nigel's activator had apparently unnerved them—it was nice to know they had nerves. According to Talps, though, our worries were far from over. Other multi-heads were being pulled off their specter worlds to add to the fray. There seemed to be an inexhaustible supply.

Nigel and I huddled in a corner. I gave him my plan.

"Why not," he asked, "use your Security Plus mechs from Happy City?"

"Not enough of 'em," I said.

He ran a thumb over his mustache. "It's risky," he told me. "There could be a direct hit on this building while we're trying to bring this off."

"We could all hide in the basement."

"What basement?"

"Yeah, you're right. But it's a chance we gotta take. It's

the quickest way to rout the enemy. And our boys will be super-trained, born fighters like their leader. And, of course, highly motivated.''

"It is a bit early for you to be patting yourself on the back," Nigel said testily.

"Credit where credit is due," I said with simple modesty. "What will they use for weapons?"

"Talps says she's got a whole batch lying around," I said. "All that Tool Works gear Spelville swiped hasn't been idle."

The Dunjers stormed across the plain.

There seemed to be thousands of 'em but that was probably too many. I'd stopped counting after the tenth. They came in all shapes and sizes; none of 'em, however, were multi-heads. But then we'd used a real activator, not one that had turned up on a specter world. Some had their own lasers, as was befitting a true Dunjer. Others were supplied with weapons from Talps's arsenal.

"There goes a proud and rugged band," I said to Nigel. "And they're all Dunjer—give or take a bit."

"I don't see you joining them," he said.

"Yeah, that's the one Dunjer missing. But they're fighting for a solid world to live on, and I've already got one. Besides, we can't all be foot soldiers, someone's got to be general. And I guess I'm the guy nominated to carry that awesome burden.''

"By whom?"

"By *me*, the chief Dunjer on the scene. You can have my autograph later—if we survive this dumb brawl."

CHAPTER 30

I was on the three hundred and fifty-second floor of the Happy City City Hall, in Mayor Strapper's temporary office, far away from the noisy repair work being done on the top floors.

"Yeah," I said, "Talps's world was well beyond the fabric of the universe. Catastrophes happen when the fabric is loused up by an activator. Being outside made her world safe from disaster."

"And our world?" Strapper asked.

"Safe, too, Mr. Mayor. She never set foot on this world. Everything was done long-distance, either psychically or through the tunnels, with the activator up in her world, sort of pulling the strings. You follow?"

"Don't be ridiculous, of course not."

"Right. After the grand Dunjer victory when all those multi-heads had been knocked off or sent into the fabric, Nigel made a couple of adjustments that fixed everything."

"Everything?"

"Uh huh. He sent the wicked Splat specters—minus their activators—back to their specter world. He closed down the tunnel from here to Talps's world, and confiscated her activator, so there'd be no more monkey business. And about returning everything that belonged here to Happy City, you already know, since you were one of the things returned.''

"Indeed I was. An unforgettable experience, Dunjer. But one I am making every effort to forget. Why in heaven's name did she kidnap the top three floors of City Hall?''

I sat back in my chair, gazed out the window. The sun shone in a clear blue sky. The multi-shaped and colored buildings were looking okay. Somehow I didn't mind their crazy-quilt appearance just now. No more gray specter skies, streets, houses, and landscapes. No more Dunjers stretching like string beans. Laura back where she belonged, namely with me. Sass out of the clink and footing the bill. And me enjoying the first peace and quiet in days. It took no getting used to at all.

"That's where you and all the administrators hang out,'' I said. "She wanted help in setting up her government. She'd already pulled a bunch of people off the specter worlds with her activator, made 'em real, but didn't know how to run a real society. You guys were the experts.''

"Surely you jest.''

"Well, that's the way it seemed to her. She was gonna return all of you later, she says.''

"How nice. Now what was this nonsense about someone here at the Hall being involved in those robberies?''

"An error. There were lots of 'em in this business. When I asked Jimmy Jimmy, the stoolie, who had set me up, he managed to whisper your name and the word 'his' before going off to his just rewards. I figured he meant something like one of your vice mayors, or deputies. I was wrong. He'd wanted to say, 'Strapper, his City Hall's gonna be pinched.' ''

"He *knew?*''

"Talps let it slip to Dr. Spelville in one of her psychic communiqués. She was no genius, just psychic. The good doctor was so shaken by this whole business, the voice in his noodle, the dough it was helping him get, the little things he had to do for the voice that didn't make sense, that he spilled the beans to his stooge, Jimmy Jimmy.''

"And then had him killed,'' Strapper said.

"Uh uh. Another error. Talps had been doing some psychic eavesdropping on me, learned I was going to brace the stoolie. She warned Spelville, who sent some boys around to make sure Jimmy kept his lip buttoned. The bomb was supposed to scare him, not do him in. but when he heard my scuffle with the thugs, he stepped out on the landing to see what was going on, and was blown away.''

"Tisk-tisk.'' Strapper stretched in his chair, smiled at me. "So what finally happened to all those Dunjers?''

"Nothing. They stayed put,'' I said. "It's their heart's desire.''

"Alone?''

I grinned at him. "Hardly alone. Before he left, Nigel scoured the specter worlds for Lauras. Came up with quite a nice crop.''

"But Dunjer, how do you know all the Dunjers will want Lauras?''

"Hell, Strapper, if *I* don't know, *who* does?''

BIO OF A SPACE TYRANT
Piers Anthony

"Brilliant...a thoroughly original thinker and storyteller with a unique ability to posit really *alien* alien life, humanize it, and make it come out alive on the page." *The Los Angeles Times*

A COLOSSAL NEW FIVE VOLUME SPACE THRILLER—
BIO OF A SPACE TYRANT
The Epic Adventures and Galactic Conquests of Hope Hubris

VOLUME I: REFUGEE   84194-0/$4.50 US/$5.50 Can
Hubris and his family embark upon an ill-fated voyage through space, searching for sanctuary, after pirates blast them from their home on Callisto.

VOLUME II: MERCENARY   87221-8/$4.50 US/$5.50 Can
Hubris joins the Navy of Jupiter and commands a squadron loyal to the death and sworn to war against the pirate warlords of the Jupiter Ecliptic.

VOLUME III: POLITICIAN   89685-0/$4.50 US/$5.50 Can
Fueled by his own fury, Hubris rose to triumph obliterating his enemies and blazing a path of glory across the face of Jupiter. Military legend...people's champion...promising political candidate...he now awoke to find himself the prisoner of a nightmare that knew no past.

VOLUME IV: EXECUTIVE   89834-9/$4.50 US/$5.50 Can
Destined to become the most hated and feared man of an era, Hope would assume an alternate identify to fulfill his dreams.

VOLUME V: STATESMAN   89835-7/$4.50 US/$5.50 Can
The climactic conclusion of Hubris' epic adventures.

THE CONTINUATION
OF THE FABULOUS
INCARNATIONS OF IMMORTALITY
SERIES

PIERS ANTHONY

FOR LOVE OF EVIL
75285-9/$4.95 US/$5.95 Can

AND ETERNITY
75286-7/$4.95 US/$5.95 Can

RETURN TO AMBER...

THE ONE *REAL* WORLD, OF WHICH ALL OTHERS, INCLUDING EARTH, ARE BUT SHADOWS

ROGER ZELAZNY

The New Amber Novel

KNIGHT OF SHADOWS   75501-7/$3.95 US/$4.95 Can
Merlin is forced to choose to ally himself with the Pattern of Amber or of Chaos. A child of both worlds, this crucial decision will decide his fate and the fate of the true world.

SIGN OF CHAOS   89637-0/$3.95 US/$4.95 Can
Merlin embarks on another marathon adventure, leading him back to the court of Amber and a final confrontation at the Keep of the Four Worlds.

The Classic Amber Series

NINE PRINCES IN AMBER	01430-0/$3.50 US/$4.50 Can
THE GUNS OF AVALON	00083-0/$3.95 US/$4.95 Can
SIGN OF THE UNICORN	00031-9/$3.95 US/$4.95 Can
THE HAND OF OBERON	01664-8/$3.95 US/$4.95 Can
THE COURTS OF CHAOS	47175-2/$3.50 US/$4.25 Can
BLOOD OF AMBER	89636-2/$3.95 US/$4.95 Can
TRUMPS OF DOOM	89635-4/$3.95 US/$4.95 Can

ARTHUR C. CLARKE'S VENUS PRIME

by Paul Preuss

VOLUME 1: BREAKING STRAIN   75344-8/$3.95 US/$4.95 CAN
Her code name is Sparta. Her beauty veils a mysterious past and
abilities of superhuman dimension, the product of advanced
biotechnology.

VOLUME 2: MAELSTROM   75345-6/$3.95 US/$4.95 CAN
When a team of scientists is trapped in the gaseous inferno of
Venus, Sparta must risk her life to save them.

VOLUME 3: HIDE AND SEEK   75346-4/$3.95 US/$4.95 CAN
When the theft of an alien artifact, evidence of extraterrestrial
life, leads to two murders, Sparta must risk her life and identity
to solve the case.

VOLUME 4: THE MEDUSA ENCOUNTER
75348-0/$3.95 US/$4.95 CAN
Sparta's recovery from her last mission is interrupted as she sets
out on an interplanetary investigation of her host, the Space
Board.

VOLUME 5: THE DIAMOND MOON
75349-9/$3.95 US/$4.95 CAN
Sparta's mission is to monitor the exploration of Jupiter's moon,
Amalthea, by the renowned Professor J.Q.R. Forester.

Each volume features a special technical infopak,
including blueprints of the structures of *Venus Prime*